MW00776359

Decision Height

Meredith Dayna Levy

A SAMUEL FRENCH ACTING EDITION

FOUNDED 1830

SAMUELFRENCH.COM
SAMUELFRENCH-LONDON.CO.UK

ISBN 978-0-573-70326-3

www.SamuelFrench.com
www.SamuelFrench-London.co.uk

FOR PRODUCTION ENQUIRIES

UNITED STATES AND CANADA
Info@SamuelFrench.com
1-866-598-8449

UNITED KINGDOM AND EUROPE
Plays@SamuelFrench-London.co.uk
020-7255-4302

Each title is subject to availability from Samuel French, depending upon
country of performance. Please be aware that *DECISION HEIGHT* may
not be licensed by Samuel French in your territory. Professional and
amateur producers should contact the nearest Samuel French office or
licensing partner to verify availability.

MUSIC USE NOTE

Licensees are solely responsible for obtaining formal written permission from copyright owners to use copyrighted music in the performance of this play and are strongly cautioned to do so. If no such permission is obtained by the licensee, then the licensee must use only original music that the licensee owns and controls. Licensees are solely responsible and liable for all music clearances and shall indemnify the copyright owners of the play(s) and their licensing agent, Samuel French, against any costs, expenses, losses and liabilities arising from the use of music by licensees. Please contact the appropriate music licensing authority in your territory for the rights to any incidental music.

IMPORTANT BILLING AND CREDIT REQUIREMENTS

If you have obtained performance rights to this title, please refer to your licensing agreement for important billing and credit requirements.

DECISION HEIGHT was first produced by Hollins University and the Hollins Playwright's Lab, and subsequently performed at Mill Mountain Theatre's Trinkle Stage in Roanoke, Virginia on January 24, 2014. The performance was directed by Ernest Zulia and the cast was as follows:

EDITH "EDDIE" HARKNELL	Susanna Young
NORMA JEAN HARRIS	Emma Sperka
ROSALIE HARTSON	Natalie Pendergast
VIRGINIA HASCALL	Russell Wilson
ALICE HAWKINS	Jeanette Florio
CAROL HENDERSON	Aileen Buckland
MRS. DEATON	Kate Dalton
ZIGGIE LEWIS	Bonnie Branch
MILDRED SIMMONS	Maggie Dwyer
ENSEMBLE	Elizabeth Hedrick, Hallie Goldberg, Cheyenne Lee Sara Peterson, Kara Wright

The production received multiple honors from the 2014 Kennedy Center American College Theatre Festival, including the Harold and Mimi Steinbeg National Student Playwriting Award, Outstanding Production of a New Work, Distinguished Achievement in Direction of a New Work, and Distinguished Ensemble Achievement. Additional honors from the 2013 Kennedy Center American College Theatre Festival include the David Shelton Full-Length Play Award and the National Partners of the American Theatre Playwriting Award.

CHARACTERS

(all female cast; listed in order of appearance)

VIRGINIA HASCALL – early 20's. The empathetic observer.

EDITH "EDDIE" HARKNELL – mid 20's. The blunt and quick witted "hot pilot."

NORMA JEAN HARRIS – late 20's. The confident teacher.

ROSALIE HARTSON – late teens/early 20's. The brave dreamer.

ALICE HAWKINS – late 20's. The cool intellect.

CAROL HENDERSON – late teens/early 20's. The brazen and earnest runt of the litter.

MRS. DEATON – late 30's/early 40's. The government-employed den mother.

ZIGGIE LEWIS – early to mid 40's. A rare woman indeed.

MILDRED SIMMONS – late 20's. A woman of few loyalties.

ENSEMBLE MEMBERS – (optional; see production notes)

SETTING

Various locations at Avenger Field, the Women Airforce Service Pilots training base, in Sweetwater, TX, including: the bay, the wishing well, the drill field, the hangar, the runway, ready room, and the class room.

TIME

November 1943 through May 1944

PRODUCTION NOTES

On "flight positions":

This script specifies that the women will occasionally "move to a flight position." This can be something as simple as a specifically lit spot on the floor. What's important is that the positions be decidedly different than other moments of standing.

On race:

Due to the climate of racism in America at this time, there was only one Chinese-American WASP. Each production should use their best judgement when colorblind casting.

On the deaths:

Mildred, Ziggie, and Norma Jean all die "in the air" so to speak. The playwright suggests a convention where the women cringe as lights flash or go out. But, there's more than one way to skin a cat.

On the radio broadcasts:

There is a radio broadcast heard in scene fourteen, specific portions of which are written in the script; the places where the women begin their commentary are indicated by a "*". They should finish their lines sequences before the next marked radio line. The link for the actual 26 March CBS World News Today broadcast (which the playwright hopes to be used in production) can be reached at this URL: (http://ia701203. us.archive.org/16/items/1944RadioNews/1944-03-26-CBSWorld-News-Today.mp3). It is part of an archive that the playwright recommends for other radio sound effects, and can be found at this URL: (http:// archive.org/details/1944RadioNews).

On the optional "Ensemble":

Past productions which have included an ensemble primarily used them to sing marching songs, aid in scene transitions, and participate in large group scenes. At the back of the script is an appendix which includes three "new" marching songs that should be used at specific transitions, should an ensemble be employed, as well as a list of recommended scenes that ensemble members might participate in.

ACKNOWLEDGEMENTS

So many people to thank: to both my undergraduate and graduate Hollins families, who tirelessly worked with me in developing this script, especially Todd Ristau, Ernie Zulia, and Bob Moss; to Gregg Henry and the Kennedy Center American College Theatre Festival, who honored this play with the David Shelton Full Length Play Award, the National Partners of the American Theatre Playwrighting Award, and the Harold and Mimi Steinberg National Student Playwriting Award; the many men and women who have worked so hard to chronicle this history, especially Nancy Parrish, for making so many primary documents available; Patricia Brooks Cope and my family, who have a large threshold for forgiveness and supported me through the ups and downs; last but not least, to the legends themselves: Odean "Deanie" Parrish, Jean Cole, Violet Cowden, Susie Bain, Elaine Harmon, Jane Doyle, Dora Strother, Teresa James, B.J. Erickson, Madge Minton, Lillian Yonally, Ann Carl, Marjorie Sandford, Dolores Reed, Kate Lee Harris, Betty Stine, Ann Berry, Ruth Adams, Nellie Henderson, Claire Siddall, Lorraine Zillner, Mary Howson, Elizabeth Johnson, and especially Mildred Davidson and Kay D'Arezzo. This play is for all of you.

TIMELINE

November 1943

Week One – Scene 1, 2

Week Two – Scene 3

Week Three – Scene 4, 5

December 1943

Week Five – Scene 6

Week Seven/Eight – Scene 7

31 December – Scene 8

January – Feburary 1944

1 January – Scene 9

Weeks Eleven–Thirteen – Scene 10

February 1944

Week Fifteen – Scene 11

March 1944

Week Seventeen – Scene 12, 13

26 March – Scene 14, 15

April 1944

Scene 16

May 1944

Last week before graduation – Scene 17, 18

Graduation Day – Scene 19, 20

You can read a lot of documents about history, but it really doesn't have the impact that the theater has because it is a vicarious experience. You are inviting the audience to experience it with you. You experience it with the spirit as well as the intellect...If a story gets told really good, it becomes your story, your experience.

– Daystar/Rosalie Jones

To fly...permanently changed one's sense of space and one's concept of what the world looks like-not only an aesthetic experience, flight was an expression of independence and free will, a triumph over the eternal static hold of Gravity

– Sally VanWagenen Keil

ACT ONE

Scene One

(We are at the wishing well, at the center of Avenger Field's campus, in Sweetwater, Texas. In history, the "wishing well" was a fountain, twenty feet in diameter and three feet tall; the walls were made of field stone.)

(Lights reveal the incoming class of 44-W-4, including **VIRGINIA, EDDIE, NORMA JEAN, ROSALIE, ALICE,** *and* **CAROL,** *in a tableau of arrival.* **VIRGINIA** *stands separate.)*

(With the entrance of **MRS. DEATON,** *the scene comes to life, and* **MRS. DEATON** *must fight to be heard over their excited chatter.)*

MRS. DEATON. Excuse me? Quiet please. May we have some quiet, please! Ladies, if you want to see the inside of a run room, and not the inside of a train car bound for home, you'll have to zip your lips!

VIRGINIA. *(addressing the audience)*

My Dearest William,

Please, do not be angry with me. When we last talked you said you would accept my leaving, if my father did, and you knew as well as I he never would. He is a pacifist.

MRS. DEATON. Since there is only one foot looker per girl in each bay, you will be allowed to store surplus baggage here in the office until arrangements are made to ship it home.

VIRGINIA. But darning socks does nothing to stop Hitler, nor will sewing patchwork quilts prevent Pearl Harbor from happening somewhere else.

MRS. DEATON. Large musical instruments and golf clubs might not be appropriate, under the circumstances.

VIRGINIA. I am capable of doing more because Jackie Cochran, the most famous woman pilot in the world, sent *me* a letter, saying a student's pilot license is all they need now.

MRS. DEATON. Welcome to Avenger Fields, home of the Women Airforce Service Pilot training program.

VIRGINIA. I can ferry planes to bases, I can test engines and tow gunning targets; I can take the place of a man, which makes him free to be over there. And the more men we have fighting, the sooner the war will end.

MRS. DEATON. The mess hall is that large building over there, the classrooms are in that direction, the flight line, ready rooms and hangars are that way. All of your bays are behind me.

VIRGINIA. I know you would join up, if they would let you.

MRS. DEATON. You'll never be lost if you can find your way back here: this fountain sits in the center of campus.

VIRGINIA. But it is not your fault that your eyes cannot see colors right.

MRS. DEATON. Most of the girls refer to it as "the wishing well" and will toss coins in before their check rides from time-to-time.

VIRGINIA. Do not give any mind to those who taunt you. I know their words sting, but they cannot know that the work you do every day is keeping their sons and husbands fed.

MRS. DEATON. I feel it is my duty to warn you now that it will take a lot more than a wish and a few pennies to graduate a WASP.

VIRGINIA. You have your work, and now I have mine. We must remain strong.

MRS. DEATON. Bays are assigned in alphabetical order…

VIRGINIA. Because I love you, madly, but we have the rest of our lives to play house, right?

MRS. DEATON. …so listen for your bay number *please*!

VIRGINIA. I hope you can find it in your heart to forgive me.

MRS. DEATON. Edith Harknell…

EDDIE. Eddie! Eddie Harknell! Edith is my grandmother.

VIRGINIA. I cannot imagine a future without you in it.

MRS. DEATON. Norma Jean Harris…

NORMA JEAN. *(in a high-class Carolinian drawl)* Present and accounted for.

VIRGINIA. Love you always…

MRS. DEATON. Rosalie Hartson

ROSALIE. Did she say Hartson? Oh Lord, that's me!

VIRGINIA. Your Virginia.

MRS. DEATON. Virginia Hascall…

VIRGINIA. *(joining the scene)* Here!

MRS. DEATON. Alice Hawkins…

ALICE. Present, ma'am.

MRS. DEATON. Carol Henderson.

CAROL. That's me! That's me!

MRS. DEATON. All of you, bay seventeen!

(Lights. The **WOMEN** *search for their bay: six cots, and six foot lookers.)*

EDDIE. Bay ten, bay eleven…dang it, how'd we get to bay five?!

NORMA JEAN. How you got to be a pilot, I only can guess.

CAROL. I see it! I see it! We're all the way at the end.

ALICE. That says twenty-seven, not seventeen. I think you need glasses, hon.

CAROL. They're packed. I was afraid they wouldn't let me in if they knew I had them.

EDDIE. *(to* **NORMA JEAN***)* See, and you think I'm bad pilot material…

ALICE. You should wear them. We don't want you to trip over a rattlesnake because you couldn't see it.

ROSALIE & VIRGINIA. There are rattlesnakes here?

CAROL. Every poisonous species that lives in the US you can find in Texas.

NORMA JEAN. Good Lord.

ALICE. It's the "Rattlesnake Capitol of the World."

EDDIE. And how do you know that?

ROSALIE. Here it is! Bay seventeen.

NORMA JEAN. Thank God. I could go for a nice hot shower…

VIRGINIA. Or a bath.

EDDIE. Sorry to say ladies, but you're not gonna find either of those here.

CAROL. Cot by the window is mine!

NORMA JEAN. Now, just hold on –

EDDIE. *(threatening a punch)* Yeah, Shrimp, 'less you wanna wash out.

*(**EDDIE** claims the cot by the window. **CAROL** in turn, claims the cot that **NORMA JEAN** wanted.)*

NORMA JEAN. Now, wait just a moment! This is my cot.

EDDIE. Shrimp, why don't you take the bed over there, the one that's saggier than all the others.

CAROL. My name is Carol!

EDDIE. You're the smallest, seems to me you've got the best chances of not touching the floor when you sleep.

VIRGINIA. That is not a very nice thing to say.

EDDIE. Army didn't hire us to be nice, Kid.

ROSALIE. *(at the farthest cot from **EDDIE**)* I think I'll take this one.

NORMA JEAN. This is my cot!

CAROL. No it's not. No it's not.

ALICE. I really think that –

EDDIE. Who died and made you Mama?

ALICE. Hey! Draw cards. The highest card wins.

EDDIE. You see a deck of cards lying around?

*(**ALICE** pulls a deck out of her pocket or purse.)*

You and I are gonna get along. Aces are low, seem fair?

NORMA JEAN. Should we draw in order of who has the most flight hours?

EDDIE. That would be me.

CAROL. How do you know?

NORMA JEAN. Or should we go alphabetically?

EDDIE. Still me. Queen.

ROSALIE. Respectable.

EDDIE. You wanna draw next?

ROSALIE. Sure. Four. Oh dear, that's bad, isn't it?

CAROL. I'll draw next! I'll draw next! Two.

NORMA JEAN. Serves you right, for making all that noise. Ace!

ALICE. Six.

VIRGINIA. King?!

| **EDDIE.** | **ALICE.** |
| Dang it! | Nice draw, honey. |

VIRGINIA. I have never won anything in my whole life.

EDDIE. Congratulations. Pick a cot.

(*MRS. DEATON enters. THE SIX scramble to stand at attention.*)

(*She carries a box of uniforms – or perhaps* **MILDRED** *or an ensemble member is carrying them for her.*)

MRS. DEATON. Hello girls.

(*The* **WOMEN** *ad-lib greetings.*)

I hope everything is to your liking. If not, tough. The latrine has two showers, two toilets, two sinks. You'll share it with Bay Eighteen next door. Now, all of you are in flight two so you'll go to school first and then fly in the afternoon –

CAROL. Excuse me, Mrs. Deaton, but did you say "school?"

MRS. DEATON. Yes, ground school. Physics, navigation and the like? Didn't think you'd just signed up to play with the planes, did you?

CAROL. No, no ma'am.

MRS. DEATON. I thought not. Curfew is at ten, on the dot. You can wear any shoes as long as they're not heels or…

(She eyes CAROL*'s cowboy boots.)*

…cowboy boots. Here are your uniforms. I'm told the women call the coveralls "zoot suits." Take note of how the other girls have adjusted them to fit their petit frames. The flight turbans are an idea by our own General Urban: to prevent any problems arising from "bad hair days." My office is in the administration building down to the right and I live in Officer Barrack One, if you need to find me.

(The WOMEN *ad-lib good-byes as* MRS. DEATON *exits.)*

ROSALIE. Oh dear. They're…

EDDIE. Big.

VIRGINIA. Really big.

CAROL. Way too big.

NORMA JEAN. They were men's suits.

EDDIE. You don't say.

ROSALIE. Ugh, still smells like them too.

NORMA JEAN. Since we've only got a half-an-hour for both bays to use the latrine in the morning, I think half of us should shower in the evenings…

*(*EDDIE *stifles a laugh.)*

Care to share with the class, Edith?

EDDIE. *(sizing her up)* It's Eddie, and I've got nothing to say… Ace.

NORMA JEAN. *(exiting)* I'm going to see if the girls in Bay Eighteen want to work out a time-chart.

ALICE. This will be a very long seven months if you keep pushing her buttons like that.

EDDIE. That's if she doesn't wash.

ALICE. Or if you don't wash.

EDDIE. I'm not gonna wash.

ROSALIE. I'm sorry, I'm not sure I understand…?

EDDIE. Wash out.

CAROL. You mean like, fail? Like…

EDDIE. Like you fail your check rides and they send you home that very minute on your own dime.

CAROL. Damn!

ALICE. *(exiting to latrine)* Carol, you're never going get your wings if you can't keep cool.

CAROL. Keep cool. Like you? I can do that.

EDDIE. Keep cool when it's eighty degrees in November? I'm gonna need some ice cream. Wanna head with me to the mess hall anyone?

ROSALIE. Are you sure? Rations –

EDDIE. Don't apply to the army. Fighting boys get butter, ice cream, and gravy, which means so do we. C'mon.

(**WOMEN** *exit.*)

Scene Two

(Lights. Civilian flight instructor, **ZIGGIE LEWIS,** *appears on the drill field.)*

(Underneath the monologue, **WOMEN** *enter to stand at attention, dressed in their zoot suits.)*

ZIGGIE. *(addressing the audience)*

Attention! Look on each side of you. One of you will be left here at the end.

No doubt you all can flit about the sky in your Piper Cubs, but to graduate a WASP, you're gonna need to learn to fly *real* planes.

You will march everywhere: to breakfast, to the flight line, to the latrine. You will keep your bays neat. Cameras are contraband. You will abstain from consuming alcohol; you will abstain from gambling. You will abstain from wandering from your cot after curfew. You will politely decline answering any invites you have to movies or dinners or the water tower from any of the locals. Not that any of them would have you.… You will fast learn here that there are men who find a woman in uniform to be… Well, the important thing is they're wrong.

Today we're going to fly PT-19's, and after two weeks some lucky lady is going to be the first to solo. You'll soon all catch up. When fifty-five hours in PT are done, we move on to advanced training with AT-6's and AT-17's, and when sixty hours there are up – around the end of March probably – we move on to basic instruments with BT-13's and take cross country solos before graduation in May. Then you become someone else's problem. I've got your instructor assignments, and where you need to report every afternoon to meet them. Any questions?

EDDIE. Yes Ma'am, just one.

ZIGGIE. What's your name, pilot?

EDDIE. Eddie. Eddie Harknell.

ZIGGIE. Permission granted, Miss Harknell, to inquire.

EDDIE. Who the hell are you?

ZIGGIE. My name is Ziggie Lewis. I'm an instructor on this base.

ROSALIE. We've got women instructors?

ZIGGIE. There's very few of us. But we're here. Now, a squadron commander and two flight lieutenants need to be nominated. Flight lieutenants will lead your flight's marches, and call you to breakfast in the morning. The Squadron Commander will, besides covering the flight lieutenants' asses, serve as the officers' liaison to the class, and play Stepmother the next seven months. Does anyone have a recommendation for Squadron Commander?

EDDIE. I recommend Norma Jean Harris!

NORMA JEAN. What?! Why me?

EDDIE. You're tall.

ZIGGIE. Does anyone second this recommendation?

NORMA JEAN. If any of you dare…

CAROL. I second!

NORMA JEAN. Shrimp!

CAROL. My name is Carol!

ZIGGIE. Do you accept this recommendation, Miss Harris?

NORMA JEAN. It's Mrs. Harris.… And yes, I'll accept.

ZIGGIE. Choose your flight lieutenants please.

(**MILDRED** *catches* **NORMA JEAN***'s eye.*)

NORMA JEAN. I recommend her.

(*to* **MILDRED**)

You are in flight one, aren't you?

MILDRED. I sure am! My name is Mildred Simmons and I –

NORMA JEAN. Fine, Mildred here can be lieutenant of flight one.

ZIGGIE. And your flight lieutenant for flight two?

NORMA JEAN. I recommend…

EDDIE. Don't look at me like that Ace, I will kill you in your sleep.

NORMA JEAN. …Alice Hawkins.

ZIGGIE. Does anyone second this recommendation?

VIRGINIA. I do.

ZIGGIE. Do you accept, Miss Hawkins?

ALICE. *(exchanging a look with* **NORMA JEAN***)* It's Mrs. Hawkins, and yes, I do.

Scene Three

(Lights. Evening in the bay. **ROSALIE** *plays "Battle Hymn of the Republic" on her flute.* **CAROL**, **ALICE**, *and* **EDDIE** *are playing poker with* **MILDRED**. **VIRGINIA** *is writing a letter.* **NORMA JEAN** *enters from the latrine.)*

NORMA JEAN. *(to* **EDDIE***)* That "Urban Turban" is only for the flight line.

EDDIE. Yeah, well it also works for wet hair.

NORMA JEAN. Speaking of which, you spent your five minutes and my five minutes in the shower. I spent my whole time worried some officer was going to come in calling lights out and catch me!

EDDIE. I see your five, and I raise you…fifty.

CAROL. She's bluffing. She's bluffing.

NORMA JEAN. What is this?

MILDRED. She's not bluffing, Eddie couldn't keep that cool on a bluff.

EDDIE. Shut your trap, Mildred.

NORMA JEAN. Is this poker?

ALICE. All in.

NORMA JEAN. You all are gambling?!

CAROL. I'm out.

MILDRED. Out too. What'd ya got, Miss H.P.?

NORMA JEAN. Who are you?

MILDRED. I'm Mildred…your flight lieutenant?

NORMA JEAN. You don't live here.

MILDRED. No, I'm over in Bay Twenty-Six.

NORMA JEAN. Then I suggest you get back to it!

MILDRED. *(salute and exit)* Yes Sir!

NORMA JEAN. It's past ten, we should all be in bed.

EDDIE. Yeah, well, tell that to Songbird over there.

ROSALIE. Who, me?

VIRGINIA. Don't mind her, Rosalie.

ROSALIE. Don't you like the song? My father taught it to me, it was his favorite as a child. I can play something else if you'd rather.

NORMA JEAN. No, darling, it's a nice song.

CAROL. Let's see those cards.

EDDIE. It's not much, just a straight. A ten-jack-queen-king-ace straight.

CAROL. Alice, Alice, please tell me you got a full house to knock her off her Sweet-Six high.

(**ALICE** *lays down her cards: she's won.*)

EDDIE. Goddammit!

NORMA JEAN.	**EDDIE**.
(*rushing at* **EDDIE**) Edith Harknell, you watch your language, I don't want to hear anything like that said in this bay ever again, do you understand me?	Ace, this is a free country and I will say what I want to, you have no right to –

NORMA JEAN. (*cutting her off, to everyone*) Time for bed!

(*As everyone prepares for bed,* **EDDIE** *pulls a cigarette and lighter out. Early in their argument,* **ROSALIE** *begins playing her flute again.*)

Where did you get this cigarette?

EDDIE. Give it back!

NORMA JEAN. I won't have any smoking in this bay. You want to smoke, you go outside!

EDDIE. Fine, I will!

NORMA JEAN. No you won't, it's after hours, you get into your cot.

EDDIE. I think someone's got a lot of hot air because of the little S.C. next to her name.

NORMA JEAN. I only got those because of you.

CAROL. And me!

NORMA JEAN & EDDIE. Go to bed, Shrimp!

CAROL. My name is Carol!

ALICE. You're all acting like children.

NORMA JEAN. I have eight-year-old students back home that listen better than she does.

EDDIE. Yeah, well, I'm not the one having a tantrum in her underwear.

NORMA JEAN. Flight Lieutenant Hawkins, you should be backing me up on this, not playing poker with the hot-pilot looking to get herself a demerit.

EDDIE. *(gesturing to ALICE)* Poker was Alice's idea.

NORMA JEAN. What?!

ALICE. We've been studying since dinner. Carol was ready to stab someone's eye out with her pencil.

NORMA JEAN.	CAROL.
Shrimp, I swear, if this is true I'll ground your behind for the rest of the week –	I was not, I was not! If you want, I can stab your eye out with a pencil.

EDDIE.	ALICE.
Shut your trap, Ace!	She's just a kid, Norma Jean!

VIRGINIA. *(standing on her cot) I am not going to stand all this bickering anymore!* I gave up a lot to get here and we all want the same thing, right? We all want this wretched war to end? How can we help do that if we are too busy squabbling like birds!

(short beat)

EDDIE. Get off your soapbox, Kid.

NORMA JEAN. Now you're going to stretch that cot out till it's worse than Shrimp's.

CAROL. For the last time, my name is –

ALICE. We all know what your name is.

VIRGINIA. I know we are all from different places, and we have different ideas on how we want all this to work, but we have got to work together at some point if we want to make it through this without dying!

ROSALIE. *(earnestly)* Or washing.

VIRGINIA. So: when I was in university, we had roommates…

CAROL. Congratulations to you.

VIRGINIA. …And each pair of roommates had to write up a contract together.

NORMA JEAN. A contract?

VIRGINIA. We had to spell everything out: when we wanted lights out, when we could practice our music…

EDDIE. Did you hear that, Songbird?

VIRGINIA. Maybe that's what we need. Maybe we should write out a contract.

ALICE. I think that's a great idea, Virginia.

VIRGINIA. You do?

NORMA JEAN. What are we going to write it on?

EDDIE. The Kid here is sitting on a ton of stationary.

CAROL. That sounds good, that's good.

NORMA JEAN. Alright, what should we call it? Contract of Bay Seventeen?

ROSALIE. That's rather dull sounding.

CAROL. On the farm we put horses that worked well together in teams. We could be like that, like a team.

NORMA JEAN. I don't like the word team.

VIRGINIA. We could be a sisterhood, or an order.

ALICE. I think sisterhood has a nice ring to it.

VIRGINIA. Marvelous, we can be the sisterhood of…of the…

EDDIE. Of the Fifinella!

ROSALIE. The little Disney gremlin above the Avenger Field sign?

EDDIE. That's the WASP mascot.

NORMA JEAN. It's not…it's not a pagan symbol, is it?

EDDIE. What about war ever struck you as Christian?

VIRGINIA. It's decided then: we are now members of the Sisterhood of the Fifinella!

ALICE. Now, what does this Sisterhood entail?

VIRGINIA. You're asking me?

ALICE. This was your idea, wasn't it?

VIRGINIA. I suppose it was.

EDDIE. What's wrong Kid, haven't you ever had an idea of your own before?

VIRGINIA. I am here, aren't I?

ALICE. So that's the first rule.

NORMA JEAN. Rules! We get to have rules!

EDDIE. You had to use the word "rules?"

ALICE. I just mean that that's the first law. We think for ourselves.

NORMA JEAN. But second, we listen to what our fellow Fifinellas have to say before we make a decision.

EDDIE. Third, we push each other to live bigger lives than we've been living.

CAROL. Fourth, we treat each other with respect, regardless of our size.

ROSALIE. Fifth, we promise to be there for each other. When we're needed.

VIRGINIA. Is there anything else?

NORMA JEAN. There are six of us, there should be six laws.

VIRGINIA. How about…we accept that we do not know everything about who we were before, and we never might, but the women we were before…they are not who we are now.

ALICE. Even though we might go back to being those women when this is over.

CAROL. Done! Let's all sign.

ALICE. We should celebrate.

ROSAL. Celebrate with what?

ALICE. *(revealing a bottle, previously hidden)* With this.

NORMA JEAN. Is that alcohol!

EDDIE. It's not cider.

VIRGINIA. How did you get that in here?

ALICE. My husband mailed it to me.

NORMA JEAN. But we're not supposed to – !

EDDIE. Law number three: live big, remember?

ROSALIE. The label is written in French.

CAROL. So? He bought her a fancy wine. Big deal.

ALICE. Roger is a BT-13 pilot. He doesn't often have time to write letters; he's not even allowed to tell me where he is half the time. So he sends me wine instead. That's how I know where he is.

(**ALICE** *opens the bottle and sips. She hands it to* **NORMA JEAN.**)

NORMA JEAN. *(she takes a sip, then –)* God forgive me.

(she takes a second sip, then a third.)

ALICE. Norma Jean, are you leaving any left in that bottle?

EDDIE. Clearly, Alice, you're not the only one who knows how to kick back.

CAROL. Yeah, Norma Jean where did you learn to do that?

NORMA JEAN. I'm a married woman too, Shrimp. There's a lot of things I know how to kick back.

(**NORMA JEAN** *realizes what she's just said;* **WOMEN** *laugh.*)

ROSALIE. Where is he?

NORMA JEAN. *(going to take another sip)* With everyone else's husband.

EDDIE. Give me that!

(She takes a sip, perhaps one too big, then turns to **CAROL.**)

Think you can handle it, Shrimp?

CAROL. If we're gonna do this, you're all gonna stop calling me Shrimp! Alright?

(Everyone agrees. **CAROL** *drinks. She not used to drinking wine, and makes a face.)*

EDDIE. Shrimp.

(**CAROL** *glowers at* **EDDIE**, *but hands it to* **ROSALIE**, *who deftly swigs.)*

ROSALIE. Mm. Very nice.

(VIRGINIA swigs, then goes to spit it out.)

EDDIE.	ALICE.
Fifinella's swallow!	Careful! It'll stain the
Fifinella's swallow!	sheets!

NORMA JEAN. Have we a virgin drinker on our hands?

ROSALIE. Don't you take communion?

VIRGINIA. We use grape juice!

EDDIE. Good. Communion wine is awful.

NORMA JEAN. I didn't take you for one who knew what communion wine tastes like.

EDDIE. If you must know, my father was a Catholic.

NORMA JEAN. Was?

EDDIE. Yeah, he wasn't one for rules either.

Scene Four

(Lights. Early next morning in the bay.)

(VIRGINIA in bed, writing.)

VIRGINIA. My darling, these past two weeks have been a blur. Here at Avenger Fields, our days are so exactly regimented, I'm lucky if I ever get a chance to look at myself in the mirror. I'm sure one day I'll look up and not recognize myself. Our day's start with morning reveille at six-fifteen.

(The reveille is heard. **NORMA JEAN** *rolls and falls out of bed. She pulls the covers off of* **EDDIE.***)*

NORMA JEAN. Get up!

EDDIE. No.

NORMA JEAN. My god, Edith, when was the last time you showered?

(she pulls the sheets off of **ALICE***)*

Don't look at me like that, Alice. We can't go eat breakfast if you don't lead the march.

(she pulls the sheets off of **CAROL***. No response.)*

Carol! Carol, wake up! Alice, come wake Carol up.

VIRGINIA. We march to breakfast, scarf down our toast and jam, and are in physical training by seven.

(The **WOMEN** *march to the drill field, singing "Yankee Doodle Pilots" to the tune of "Yankee Doodle.")*

WOMEN.
WE ARE YANKEE DOODLE PILOTS
YANKEE DOODLE, DO OR DIE!
REAL LIVE NIECES OF OUR UNCLE SAM
BORN WITH A YEARNING TO FLY.
KEEP IN STEP TO ALL OUR CLASSES
MARCH TO FLIGHT LINE WITH OUR PALS.
YANKEE DOODLE CAME TO TEXAS
JUST TO FLY THE PT-S!
WE ARE THOSE YANKEE DOODLE GALS!

NORMA JEAN. Push-ups. Go.

  (Everyone drops and gives five.)

  Jumping Jacks. Go.

  (Everyone gives five.)

  Squats. Go.

  (No one but **MILDRED** *squats.)*

  I said SQUATS! GO!

  (Everyone squats.)

VIRGINIA. For the rest of the morning, we're in classes, learning everything from aerodynamics to mathematics.

  (Lights. The **WOMEN** *are in ground school; they address the audience.)*

EDDIE. There's a reason I didn't stay in school.

MILDRED. Dear Aunt Susan: I am doing well here at Cochran's convent…

CAROL. I can't remember how to do long division.

ALICE. *(raising her hand)* Seventeen knots. Five kilometers. Sixty gallons.

MILDRED. We call it that because Jackie Cochran has practically made us don a habit.

ROSALIE. The blue wire connects here, the yellow one goes there…

NORMA JEAN. So all we really need to worry about knowing is that hot air rises, and cold air sinks?
  You're telling me that God's amazing creation of nature and weather boils down to that?

MILDRED. However, if she wanted us to stay chaste, she shouldn'tve hired such good looking mechanics. Hernandez is my favorite.

CAROL. How many fives are there in 3,725?…damn it.

EDDIE. I didn't stay in school because I don't do well with books. Or rules of any kind.

ALICE. *(raising her hand)* Two hundred miles per hour. Twenty-three knots, depending on the wind.

ROSALIE. …Oh dear, I've forgotten where the red wire goes.

EDDIE. Something tells me that if I'm in school for the military, there's gonna be a lot of rules.

*(A bell rings. **ALL** exit, **CAROL** with her nose still in her book.)*

VIRGINIA. And then, in the afternoons, we fly. We all have different civilian instructors. Alice has "the mad Russian," a man who's fond of knocking the control stick against his trainee's knees; Carol instructor has not yet figured out she wears prescription goggles. Norma Jean and I have a man named Jimmy Ray, who is wonderfully patient. But Rosalie and Eddie have the legend herself.

*(Lights. **EDDIE** and **ROSALIE** in cockpits.)*

*(**ZIGGIE** is teaching.)*

ZIGGIE. Have you completed your checklist, Rosalie?

ROSALIE. Oh yes.

ZIGGIE. Then how come *this* isn't on?

ROSALIE. Oh dear. That's bad, isn't it?

VIRGINIA. Ziggie wasn't lying when she said we would learn to fly *real planes*. These military planes are much more sophisticated than the Piper Cubs we're used to. We are mostly flying PT-19's, which are something special. They have an open cockpit, and it can be easy to get carried away.

EDDIE. Whooooooooiieee!

ZIGGIE. Too high, too fast!

EDDIE. What'd you say?

ZIGGIE. I said too high, too fast!

EDDIE. Higher and Faster? Can do, boss!

VIRGINIA. Although, some of us have taken to flying them faster than others.

ROSALIE. I can't, I can't do it.

ZIGGIE. C'mon Rosie, pull the plane up.

ROSALIE. I'm not strong enough.

ZIGGIE. Yes you are!

ROSALIE. The plane is too big!

ZIGGIE. Rosalie, you're gonna run outta runway!

(**ROSALIE** *lets go of the control stick and* **ZIGGIE** *quickly pulls the plane up.*)

ZIGGIE. And that, young lady, is why we have you doing chin ups every morning.

VIRGINIA. Each day brings a new lesson. And they're not always about flying.

ZIGGIE. Eddie Harknell, don't you touch that control stick until I say so!

EDDIE. How else am I gonna learn to fly this bucket of bolts?

ZIGGIE. Same way your mother Lilly learned how. By listening to her instructor.

EDDIE. You knew my Mama?

ZIGGIE. Honey, there aren't that many of us, but everyone knew Lilly Harknell, and her sass.

(*Lights.*)

VIRGINIA. One of the upper class girls told me that whoever is first in her flight to solo – fly without an instructor – gets dumped into the wishing well by her bay mates.

(*Lights.* **NORMA JEAN, ALICE,** *and* **CAROL** *cross stage.*)

ALICE. I'd prefer to not be tossed into that fountain, thank you.

(**NORMA JEAN** *agrees.*)

CAROL. Why not? Why not? It's tradition!

NORMA JEAN. It's silly.

NORMA JEAN & ALICE. And we're too old.

VIRGINIA. By the time it's lights out, we have fallen asleep before our head even touches the pillow.
I'm exhausted, and I miss you during every second of it. Please write soon – If I knew more about how your days are, you wouldn't feel so far away. Love you, Virginia.

(Lights. **ZIGGIE, MILDRED, EDDIE,** *and* **ROSALIE** *enter marching.)*

WOMEN.

I WANNA BE A MISS H.P.

H'MMMMMM AND A LIL BIT MORE!

ROSALIE. What does H. P. mean?

WOMEN.

I WANNA BE A WASP TRAINEE,

H'MMMMMM AND A LIL BIT MORE!

EDDIE. It means Hot Pilot. You been living under a rock?

WOMEN.

I WANNA BE A GRADUATE, AND THEN I'LL ASK NO MORE!

FOR ALL I'LL HAVE ALL THAT'S COMING TO ME

H'MMMMMM AND A LIL BIT

H'MMMMMM AND A LIL BIT

H'MMMMMM AND A LIL BIT MORE!

*(***WOMEN** *march off, leaving* **EDDIE** *and* **ROSALIE** *at the well.)*

Scene Five

(Lights. Late afternoon. **EDDIE, ROSALIE,** *and* **VIRGINIA** *are at the well.* **EDDIE** *is smoking.)*

ROSALIE. I hope to be as good a pilot as Ziggie one day.

EDDIE. She's one tough cookie, I'll give her that.

VIRGINIA. What is it like, to have a woman instructor?

ROSALIE. It's helpful.

VIRGINIA. What do you mean?

ROSALIE. Well, the top ten percent of us are going to stand out really well. So will the bottom ten percent. But the majority of us are average –

EDDIE. Speak for yourself, Songbird…

ROSALIE. …and so the instructors might fall back on personal prejudice to weed some of us out. You know some of those male officers will judge us on how our hair's tucked in our turbans.

VIRGINIA. I think they're trained to look past things like that.

ROSALIE. Sometimes I have a hard time getting past *my* prejudices.

VIRGINIA. Like men?

ROSALIE. They spoil my day.

EDDIE. Well, I never had girlfriends growing up. All of my brothers' friends were my friends.

VIRGINIA. What does he think of you being here?

EDDIE. Ricky? He's all for it. Before the war, he and I barnstormed around the country for three years, picking up passengers for a penny a pound.

ROSALIE. Your folks let you do that?

EDDIE. Mama was dead and Daddy was long gone, who was gonna tell us no?

ROSALIE. Where is your brother now?

EDDIE. Flying a bomber over Germany somewhere.

NORMA JEAN. *(entering)* She did it! Alice did it! Alice flew solo!

ROSALIE & VIRGINIA.	EDDIE.
Marvelous! That's wonderful! Did she really?	Dang it! I was supposed to be first! Ziggie was gonna let me go tomorrow!

NORMA JEAN. *(to EDDIE)* That's what you said yesterday.

EDDIE. Yeah, well, it's complicated.

ROSALIE. *(to NORMA JEAN)* Eddie insulted an officer behind his back, in front of Ziggie. She called him an "ass."

EDDIE. I was just telling the truth.

CAROL. *(entering, with a camera)* Where is she? Where is she?

NORMA JEAN. Where did you get that camera?

CAROL. Are you going to take it from me?

NORMA JEAN. Not today.

CAROL. It's Alice's. She'll thank me for this later.

VIRGINIA. I always thought Alice would get in the air first. She's just brilliant.

EDDIE. It takes more than book-smarts to stay up in the air, Kid.

(ALICE enters.)

CAROL. There she is!

ROSALIE.	NORMA JEAN.
Oh Alice, what was it like? Was it just the most incredible feeling?	I knew when I chose you as my flight lieutenant, I chose the right woman!

CAROL.	VIRGINIA.
Tell us all about it, tell us all about it!	I knew it'd be you who soloed first!

ALICE. It was nice.

CAROL. It was nice? That's it!

EDDIE. You're gonna get it now.

(They drag ALICE to the well, despite her protests.)

CAROL. Say cheese!

(*CAROL snaps a picture, as* ALICE *gets pushed into the water. Cheers.*)

ALICE. Quit your hollering. It'll be you tomorrow, and if not tomorrow then the next day.

(*Lights.* ZIGGIE *in a separate spot.*)

ZIGGIE. Why do you fly? Do you love heights? Do you love speed?

(*CAROL gives* VIRGINIA *the camera, and runs to cannonball into the well.*)

CAROL. Yaaaaaaa-hhhooooooo!

ZIGGIE. Do you enjoy pretending to be one of God's angels, soaring up and around the clouds?

NORMA JEAN. If Heaven doesn't look like this, then I don't want to go.

(*NORMA JEAN steps in gracefully.*)

ZIGGIE. Are you attempting to escape a small life?

(*ROSALIE jumps in.*)

Do you fly to see what's beyond the horizon?

ALICE. I had a feeling.

ZIGGIE. Do you fly because you feel heavy?

(*EDDIE, skeptical from the sidelines, now suddenly runs and throws herself in.*)

Are you seeking another kind of baptism?

(*VIRGINIA places the camera down, and teeters on the edge.*)

VIRGINIA. I'm not, I don't know if, oh!

(*She falls in.*)

That was marvelous.

(*ZIGGIE takes a picture of their erupting celebration. Perhaps a tableau?*)

Scene Six

(Lights. Afternoon in the bay. **VIRGINIA** *decorates in preparation for Christmas.)*

*(***ROSALIE*** *plays her flute, the same "Battle Hymn of the Republic" tune.* **EDDIE** *and* **CAROL** *play poker.)*

VIRGINIA. Ida got a pink slip yesterday. Her third one.

CAROL. Did she wash?

VIRGINIA. No one has seen her since yesterday. I heard she got Captain Pinkerton.

EDDIE. You mean Captain Maytag?

CAROL. Maytag? Like the washing machine?

ROSALIE. Because he's washed out so many girls.

EDDIE. Thin, blonde, thinks he's God's Gift to Women. The ass.

VIRGINIA. She is the fifth washout this week, and it is only Wednesday.

EDDIE. The Army Way isn't for everyone.

ROSALIE. It might not have been her fault. What if her instructor just didn't like her?

CAROL. They fixed it so that can't happen. If you get a pink slip you go on a check-ride with a different civie instructor. If you get fail that, they send you up with an officer. You fail that, then they send you home.

EDDIE. On your own dime.

VIRGINIA. What is wrong, Rosalie? You look miserable.

CAROL. Are you sick or something?

EDDIE. You got pink-slipped, didn't you? Songbird's got a case of the "check-its."

VIRGINIA. Eddie!

EDDIE. What?

ROSALIE. I heard some of the upper class girls singing today. To this tune, they were singing:

WHEN WE LEAVE AVENGER, WE WILL ALL SIT DOWN AND CRY

WHEN WE LEAVE AVENGER, WE WILL ALL SIT DOWN AND
CRY
WHEN WE LEAVE AVENGER, WE WILL ALL SIT DOWN AND –

(**ROSALIE**, *overcome, cannot continue.*)

VIRGINIA. Rosalie, did you get pink slipped?

(**ROSALIE** *nods, then starts to leave the cabin.*)

Rosalie, wait.

(**NORMA JEAN** *and* **ALICE** *enter in street clothes, laden with shopping bags, blocking* **ROSALIE**'*s escape.*)

NORMA JEAN. We've returned from the great outside world!

EDDIE. *(aside)* Sweetwater is hardly great.

ALICE. It's so gray outside. I think we'll see snow before Christmas.

NORMA JEAN. Rosalie, are you feeling okay, darling? You're looking pale.

VIRGINIA. She's –

ROSALIE. I'm fine. What did you buy?

NORMA JEAN. Well, I figured that it's been a while since James has seen me in one of these...

(She pulls out two slips out of the bag.)

...So I'm going to send him a little reminder, courtesy of Alice's camera.

ALICE. I'll mail them home to my mother to get them developed.

NORMA JEAN. Which one should I put on first, Rosalie?

ROSALIE. *(points to one)* Hmm... This one.

NORMA JEAN. Virginia?

VIRGINIA. *(points to the other)* That one.

NORMA JEAN. Eddie, what do you think?... Right. You're not talking to me. Again.

EDDIE. You turned me in!

NORMA JEAN. Now you sound like a child. The rule is we're all supposed to go to a church on Sunday.

CAROL. Eddie's allergic to rules.

EDDIE. We shouldn't haveta go, and you didn't haveta turn me in.

NORMA JEAN. I did have to, Edith, it's my job as Squadron Commander to make sure that the rules –

EDDIE. Between the demerit I got for chewing out Captain Maytag last week and the demerit for my flask being found the week before, I'm grounded now the next four weeks. I'm stuck here until New Years, and if I get another demerit they're threatening to e-ride me.

ALICE. I really don't think they will give you an elimination ride for demerits.

EDDIE. Yeah, well I wouldn't put it past them. Some of those officers can't stand the fact that we women are flying the same planes as their precious God-damn male cadets!

NORMA JEAN. Don't take the Lord's name in vain like that! I don't care if you are an atheist, don't say that!

ROSALIE. Norma Jean! Don't go around accusing people of being atheists.

EDDIE. No, she's right. I don't believe in God. I do, however, believe in vows. And that's what I thought the sisterhood was about, Ace. We vowed to make our own decisions, didn't we? Think our own thoughts?

NORMA JEAN. I'm bound by a vow too, Edith, you know that.

EDDIE. I also know you're gonna let Alice use a camera – you bound to turn her in, too?

NORMA JEAN	**EDDIE**. *(mumbling in response)*
I didn't have a choice, Edith, because Mildred was the one who told me she saw you hanging around the runway, 'stead of going with her to the Catholic service like you told me,	I see, well, go ahead Ace, make excuses for yourself, that's fine, that's fine.
so I had to report it, otherwise you know she would've said something herself. I'm sorry, I really am, I wish –	

(**EDDIE** *blows cigarette smoke in her face.*)

ALICE. Why don't you try on a slip, Norma Jean. We want James to have his Christmas gift, don't we?

(**NORMA JEAN** *exits to the latrine to change.*)

EDDIE. Who are you writing, Kid?

VIRGINIA. No one.

ROSALIE. "No one" gets an awful lot of letters.

EDDIE. C'mon, Virginia.

VIRGINIA. Well, I write to lots of people. My mother, my uncle George…

ROSALIE. No siblings?

VIRGINIA. No.

EDDIE. How about a sweetheart?

VIRGINIA. I write him too.

CAROL. You have a sweetheart! How come we've never heard about him?

NORMA JEAN. *(entering)* How come we've never heard about yours?

CAROL. Mine! How did you know about mine?

NORMA JEAN. I didn't, I just said that to see what you'd say.

(in regards to the slip)

What do we think?

EDDIE. That one is nice, if you want to look twelve.

(**NORMA JEAN** *exits to the latrine to change into the second slip.*)

Don't look at me like that, Alice. She asked.

CAROL. *(to* **VIRGINIA***)* If you tell me about yours, I'll tell you about mine!

VIRGINIA. You first.

CAROL. His name is Ben. He's in the Navy, fighting in Japan. He used to work on my father's farm. He first kissed me at the rodeo after he'd stayed on a bull a whole eight seconds.

EDDIE. He sounds like quite the fella.

CAROL. I haven't heard from him in a few weeks.... Let's talk about yours, Virginia.

VIRGINIA. I don't know that he's "mine" anymore.

EDDIE. You get a Dear Jane letter or something?

VIRGINIA. Oh no, nothing like that: he and my father did not want me to come do this. I was supposed to get married in December. In fact, I was supposed to get married yesterday.

ROSALIE. You broke your engagement to come here?

VIRGINIA. No! He had agreed, hypothetically, to postponing the wedding. I do not think he was expecting me to go through with it, though. I have been sending letters since I got here, but he has not written back yet.

ALICE. What do your folks think?

CAROL. I bet your mother's furious, isn't she? My stepmother is furious.

VIRGINIA. My father certainly is, but my mother is secretly thrilled. When I was little, we would drive to the airport every Sunday after church, just the two of us, and watch the planes fly in.
    We would bring a picnic lunch and sit on the hood of our car outside the airfield and watch them, like we were watching a baseball game.

EDDIE. Isn't that adorable.

ALICE. I meant, how do your folks feel about your engagement?

VIRGINIA. Oh. Mother admitted once she thinks I am too young to be getting married, but I am twenty-two, which is the same age as she was when she got married. How old where you when you and Roger got married?

ALICE. Roger and I are not William and you. That's like comparing B-26's to Piper Cubs.

VIRGINIA. What does that mean?

ALICE. It means your mother might be right.

EDDIE. What your mother thinks doesn't matter. It's your sweetheart who's gotta get used to the idea of you flying, not her.

NORMA JEAN. *(entering)* He'll come around, you'll see. My James did.

ROSALIE. Oh, yes, that's the one, Norma Jean.

NORMA JEAN. You think so?

ROSALIE. I do. Let's take this picture.

> *(**NORMA JEAN** climbs onto the cot. **CAROL** turns on the radio, which plays "Keep Me In Your Dreams," or something of similar sentiment.)*

VIRGINIA. What do you mean, your James came around?

NORMA JEAN. We were both in college, and I was walking across the quad when I heard this very good looking young man telling some of his buddies about how he was going to apply to the Civilian Pilot Training Program. I'd been looking for a way to talk with him for weeks…

ROSALIE. Do Marie McDonald!

NORMA JEAN. *(assuming the pose)* …so I walked over and I told him I was interested in applying too, because I had always loved Amelia Earhart as a child.

ROSALIE. Ava Gardner!

NORMA JEAN. He just rolled his eyes, said that I shouldn't waste my time applying, I'd only be disappointed. So I ripped the application out of his hand and filled it out. I'll never forget the look on James' face when I walked into that classroom the first day.

ROSALIE. Betty Grable!

MILDRED. *(entering)* Hey girls, we got some of your mail by mista – oh!

> *(**MILDRED** covers her eyes, embarrassed.)*

> *(**EDDIE** gets up and takes the mail.)*

EDDIE. Shrimp, you got one from a Beth Henderson.

CAROL. That's my little sister.

EDDIE. I thought that was Ann.

CAROL. She's my other little sister. Then there's the boys: Lee, Tom and Ted.

EDDIE. How do you keep 'em all straight?

CAROL. I just call them all "monster."

EDDIE. Kid, it looks like you got one from, does that say William? I don't know, it's a little smudged...

VIRGINIA. Give me that!

NORMA JEAN.	ROSALIE.
Isn't it about time.	I bet he's writing to beg your forgiveness.

EDDIE.	CAROL.
I'd wait a week to write him back Kid, let him sweat it out a little.	What'd he say?! What'd he say?!

VIRGINIA. He wants to see me when I come home for Christmas.

NORMA JEAN. Not before?

ROSALIE. Doesn't he know he can come visit you on the weekend?

CAROL. If you're not grounded like Eddie, of course.

VIRGINIA. He has to work.

ALICE. Why isn't he serving?

VIRGINIA. They won't take him, he is colorblind.

NORMA JEAN. Eddie, what's your mouth looking like that for? Shut it up, you'll draw flies.

(She sees the look on EDDIE's face.)

Is that a telegram for – [me]? No. No. No, no, no. [I can't, you read it].

EDDIE. (reading telegram) The Army Air Force deeply regrets to inform you that your husband James Harris First Sergeant is missing following action in the performance of his duty and in the service of his country the Army Air Force appreciates your great anxiety and will furnish you further information promptly when received.

NORMA JEAN. James is missing?

EDDIE. That's what it says.

NORMA JEAN. They don't know if he's dead or if he's…

EDDIE. They don't know.

(**NORMA JEAN** *lets out a giggle, and then another. Giggles soon turn into sobs.* **NORMA JEAN** *tries to run out of the bay, but* **EDDIE** *holds her back by.*)

EDDIE.	**NORMA JEAN**.
Stop, Ace, stop it, where are you – just c'mere!	Let me go, let me go Eddie, let me…go…

(**EDDIE** *manages to embrace* **NORMA JEAN** *for a moment.* **NORMA JEAN** *then breaks away and exits, followed closely by* **ALICE**. *The others are left alone as "Keep Me in Your Dreams" continues to play.*)

Scene Seven

(Lights. **WOMEN** *march on the drill field, singing lyrics from "Gee Ma, I Want to Go Home.")*

WOMEN.

THE ARMY COTS THAT THEY GIVE US, THEY SAY ARE MIGHTY FINE,

THEY'RE NOT FOR BEAUTY RESTING, BUT STRAIGHTENING OUT THE SPINE

OH, I DON'T WANT NO MORE OF ARMY LIFE

GEE MA, I WANT TO GO HOME!

THE AIRPLANES THAT THEY GIVE US, THEY SAY ARE MIGHTY FINE,

THE DARN THINGS CAN'T SHOOT STAGES, THEY WILL NOT HIT THE LINE

OH, I DON'T WANT NO MORE OF ARMY LIFE

GEE MA, I WANT TO GO HOME!

(The **WOMEN** *stand at attention.* **NORMA JEAN** *enters.)*

NORMA JEAN. Push-ups. Go.

(Everyone drops and gives five.)

Jumping Jacks. Go.

(Everyone gives five.)

Squats. Go.

(No one but **MILDRED** *squats.)*

I said SQUATS! GO!

(Everyone squats.)

WOMEN.

THE COFFEE THAT THEY GIVE US, THEY SAY IS MIGHTY FINE

IT'S GOOD FOR CUTS AND BRUISES, AND TASTES LIKE IODINE,

OH, I DON'T WANT NO MORE OF ARMY LIFE

GEE, MA, I WANT TO GO HOME!

*(***WOMEN*** freeze, except* **VIRGINIA** *and* **ROSALIE**.*)*

ROSALIE. *(holding a pink slip)* I'm going to wash.

VIRGINIA. What are you talking about, you can fly just as well as any of us.

ROSALIE. It's one thing, flying with another civvie, but when you a second one of these – ! (*gesturing to pink slip*) – they put you up in the air with an officer, and all he'll do is stare at me. Oh, last time I could hardly breathe.

VIRGINIA. You won't pass if you stop breathing, Rosalie.

ROSALIE. The last few weeks, all I can think about is that because I came here, I've sent a boy overseas, and if I wash...what if that boy that I helped send to the Pacific is dying right now, if I wash his death will be for nothing...

VIRGINIA. Slow down. You passed last week's check ride – it will be the same today.

ROSALIE. But to do it again! I can't keep food down; I didn't sleep a wink last night.

VIRIGINIA. (*handing her a coin*) Sounds like you could use a little luck then. Take my penny.

(**ROSALIE** *takes coin and exits. Exercises resume.*)

WOMEN.

THE ZOOT SUITS THAT THEY GIVE US, THEY SAY ARE MIGHTY FINE,

YOU KEEP RIGHT ON MARCHING, AND THEY MOVE ALONG BEHIND

OH, I DON'T WANT NO MORE OF ARMY LIFE

GEE, MA, I WANT TO GO HOME!

(**WOMEN** *freeze, except* **ALICE** *and* **CAROL**.)

CAROL. Alice? How is it you always know all the answers?

ALICE. I studied physics in college. (*short beat.*) Didn't you go to college?

CAROL. My stepmother doesn't believe in women going to college. My pa believes what my stepmother tells him to.

ALICE. What's your real ma think?

CAROL. I don't know, she's gone.

ALICE. If you didn't go to school, how did you get you private license?

CAROL. I took lessons at the air field couple hours away. I paid for it all myself, teaching kids how to ride horses. It was less than college, you see, and I needed to get out of Oklahoma.

ALICE. I'll tutor you.

CAROL. I don't need tutoring.

ALICE. Fine.

CAROL. But I guess I'd like some… I don't wanna wash, Alice.

(Exercises resume.)

WOMEN.

THE QUIZZES THAT THEY GIVE US, THEY SAY ARE MIGHTY FINE,

WE NEVER KNOW THE ANSWERS, WE'RE MIXED UP ALL THE TIME,

OH, I DON'T WANT NO MORE OF ARMY LIFE

GEE MA, I WANT TO GO HOME!

(They take a break.)

VIRGINIA. I am tired. I am sick of grits and I am sick of gravy. And I don't see how squats will make me a better pilot.

NORMA JEAN. Kid, we never had it so good.

EDDIE. Yeah, a roof over our heads, three squares a day, and a loaf of pumpernickel.

ROSALIE. *(entering)* I passed! By the seat of my pants, but I passed!

(Cheers. Exercises resume.)

WOMEN.

BUT MOMMA DEAR, THE TRUTH IS, WE KNOW IT'S MIGHTY FINE,

WE LOVE IT ALL, NO KIDDING, WE THINK IT IS SUBLIME,

OH, WE STILL WANT SOME MORE OF ARMY LIFE

NO, MA, WE'RE NOT COMING HOME!

(**MILDRED** *exits.*)

NORMA JEAN. Did anybody feel that? A sharp, cold, thing hit my forehead.

CAROL. Look! Look!

NORMA JEAN. It's snow! Honest to goodness snow!

VIRGINIA. Let's get inside, before it gets too cold.

EDDIE. I'm not going in, I've never seen snow!

ROSALIE. Fine.

NORMA JEAN. Me either.

ALICE. Fine.

CAROL. Me either.

VIRGINIA. Fine.

(Lights. **MRS. DEATON** *enters with a PA microphone. Perhaps "I'll be home for Christmas" underscores.)*

MRS. DEATON. There is nearly a foot of snow on the ground in Sweetwater, Texas! Truly a Christmas Eve miracle! The good news is that you now will have five days off instead of three for Christmas, but the bad news is "Pop", the gentleman in town who owns the car garage, is refusing to release any of your cars, out of concern for your personal safety. So come on down to the gym girls! We've got a Christmas tree and fruitcake!

*(***MRS. DEATON*** exits. Lights. A spirited snowball fight erupts between the* **WOMEN**.*)*

EDDIE. This is the best Christmas I've ever had.

VIRGINIA. Me too.

ALICE. Don't let William hear you say that.

VIRGINIA. Oh. William. He is going to be very angry with me.

ROSALIE. He shouldn't be. You can't control the weather.

CAROL. Yeah, we can blame the impending cold front from Northwest Canada for that.

NORMA JEAN. Shh, listen.

(The faint sound of carolers is heard singing "Silent Night.")

Scene Eight

(Lights. New Years Eve. **EDDIE** *and* **VIRGINIA** *are walking back from the hangar.)*

EDDIE. So here I am, sweating bullets while we land, sure that he's gonna tell me to pack up my bags and go home, I washed out of primary, but instead he says to me:

(in a flirty voice)

Did you know that two "ee's" at the end of a word, for instance, "trainee," in most romance languages is oftentimes a feminine word?

VIRGINIA. He did not!

EDDIE. He did! And I say: No, Lieutenant Reinhart, sir, I was not aware of that. You see, I didn't study romance languages. Then he asks me what I did study and I say: Not much of anything, except flying. Then he winks, signs my pass slip and yells at me to get out of the plane!

VIRGINIA. Are you going to see him at the New Years Eve party tonight?

EDDIE. C'mon Virginia, you know the rules.

VIRGINIA. I know you like to break them.

EDDIE. Can you believe it? Tomorrow begins a whole new year.

VIRGINIA. And we are going to be starting it flying AT-Sweet-Sixes!

NORMA JEAN. *(entering)* She's gone!

EDDIE. Who's gone?

NORMA JEAN. I got a list of all the girls going onto advanced. Dozens of girls washed, dozens. Rosalie's name isn't on the list. She washed. She had Captain Maytag and he washed her.

VIRGINIA. We have to catch her, we have to say goodbye –

NORMA JEAN. She's already moved out of our bay, she could be anywhere.

VIRGINIA. No. We all know exactly where she is.

*(Lights. **ROSALIE** with her suitcase and flute box at the well. She steps into the water. The **WOMEN** enter.)*

What are you doing in the well? That water is freezing!

ROSALIE. It's not frozen.

NORMA JEAN. It's close enough! Get out of there.

ROSALIE. I can't. I came here to be a part of the war – I helped send a boy over there, and now he's probably dead and I'm being sent home? I'd rather die than go back home and darn socks!

EDDIE. Suicide by hypothermia isn't patriotic, Songbird, it's just stupid.

ROSALIE. Oh, why do you have this absurd need to nick-name everybody?

NORMA JEAN. Yes, Edith, keep your mouth shut.

ALICE. Rosalie, didn't you go to school for music?

ROSALIE. I didn't graduate. I came here instead.

ALICE. Now you can go back.

CAROL. Bring music to the masses! Teach little children in the cornfields of Iowa!

ROSALIE. It'll never be enough. It's not flying. Iowa isn't Sweetwater. None of you will be there.

*(**VIRGINIA** joins **ROSALIE** in the water.)*

*(to **VIRGINIA**)*

What are you – ?!

VIRGINIA. *(singing, wading toward **ROSALIE**)*
WHEN THE WAR IS OVER, WE WILL ALL FLY CUBS AGAIN
WHEN THE WAR IS OVER,

VIRIGNIA & ROSALIE.
WE WILL ALL FLY CUBS AGAIN
WHEN THE WAR IS OVER, WE WILL ALL FLY CUBS –

*(**VIRGINIA** holds **ROSALIE**. The weight of **ROSALIE**'s imminent departure is suddenly on all their shoulders.)*

ROSALIE. How am I supposed to say goodbye?

VIRGINIA. Don't say goodbye. Say…

CAROL. Sayonara!

>*(to everyone)*

What? Ben's taught me some Japanese.

>**(ROSALIE** *laughs. Everyone laughs. One by one, the* **WOMEN** *step into the water, embracing* **ROSALIE.***)*

End of Act One

ACT TWO

Scene Nine

(Lights. Just past midnight on New Years Day.)

*(**NORMA JEAN** and **VIRGINIA** in the bay.)*

NORMA JEAN. I told them to be back by 11 o'clock, at the latest. We are twenty-three minutes into 1944 and they are still not back yet.

VIRGINIA. Maybe they are on their way back now.

NORMA JEAN. We are talking about Eddie, Alice, Carol, and God-knows who all else cramming together to play poker in Mildred's latrine. And Eddie brought that garbage whisky along with her.

VIRGINIA. Maybe they feel safe, with all the officers tired out from the New Years Eve party down at the gym –

NORMA JEAN. If they think that those officers will fail to do an after-bed check tonight because they're tired out from a little party, which ended twenty-four minutes ago, they don't know anything about how the Army Air Force works. They're watching Mildred like a hawk, too, ever since her bay mate Wendy washed last week for drinking; Mrs. Deaton threatened to wash the whole bay if they didn't fess up to whose liquor it was they'd spilled all over the floor.

VIRGINIA. Is it true that she slipped and fell on it when she came in for the after-bed check?

NORMA JEAN. She fell twice. And she was livid, and they've been doubly careful with after-bed checks since. I swear, Eddie is as ungrateful as she is careless, she's just asking to get kicked out herself, and after Rosalie... If they get caught, I swear, I'm gonna....

VIRGINIA. I don't understand. Rosalie was good enough to get here in the first place.

NORMA JEAN. Darling, that doesn't mean she was good enough to stay.

VIRGINIA. She just needed more time.

NORMA JEAN. Some people are just meant for different things.

VIRGINIA. That is easy for us to say. We are still here... Any word about James?

NORMA JEAN. No, nothing yet.

VIRGINIA. How do you stand it? I know exactly where Will is, and his silence is unbearable, and then there is you, who don't even know where he...how do you stand it?

NORMA JEAN. I study radio maps. I look for shapes in the clouds, or messages. I pray. Mostly, I pray.

VIRGINIA. I'm not sure God hears my prayers. My earthly father never listened, anyway.

NORMA JEAN. I like to think of God as being a woman.

VIRGINIA. What?

NORMA JEAN. Like one of the women in my church's choir that can sing the sweetest melodies you've ever heard. With bosoms so soft they're like pillows that you know will hold even your heaviest tears. A God who will love you no matter how many times you fail Her, no matter how many times you fall short.

VIRGINIA. Norma Jean, the Bible says "He."

NORMA JEAN. Who wrote the bible, Virginia?

CAROL. *(entering)* Norma Jean! Norma Jean!

ALICE. *(entering)* SHHHH! CAROL! Are you trying to wake up the whole base?

NORMA JEAN. What in the Lord's good name are you making such a racket for?

ALICE. Mrs. Deaton's doing an after-bed check.

NORMA JEAN. What? Did she see you?

EDDIE. *(entering, spilling things)* They saw me. They, whoopsie, Mildred, I was winning and then –

NORMA JEAN. Get into bed, all of you. Eddie, pick up those chips! Hide that flask!

(to ALICE)

Do they know you were playing cards?

ALICE. I don't think so.

CAROL. I stuffed the deck down my bra!

EDDIE. What are you going to tell them?

NORMA JEAN. Oh, Eddie, did you brush your teeth with whiskey? Get yourself into bed!

EDDIE. What are you going to tell them?

NORMA JEAN. What do you mean, what am I going to tell them?

EDDIE. If you talk, Norma Jean, they'll take one look at me and wash me! They washed Wendy last week for drinking, and her uncle's a Supreme Court justice! I'm nobody, they won't even –

(knocking at the door)

What are you going to tell them?!

NORMA JEAN. Edith Harknell, if you know what is good for you, you'll get your tan, Floridian ass into your godsdammed bed, or, Lord help me I will –

(EDDIE flies into bed as MRS. DEATON and MILDRED enter. NORMA JEAN feigns just waking up.)

NORMA JEAN. I'm sorry, Mrs. Deaton, *(yawn, whispering)* is everything alright?

MRS. DEATON. Squadron Commander Harris, this young woman says three of your bay mates were with her in the latrine betwixt bay 25 and 26, not even five minutes ago.

NORMA JEAN. Well, that's odd, because my baymates and I have been sleeping for the last few hours.

MRS. DEATON. Are you sure they didn't sneak out while you were asleep?

MILDRED. That one is breathing hard.

NORMA JEAN. Edith? She's ah, got bad lungs. You should've heard her last week when she had a cold, you'd of thought a train was coming through.

MILDRED. Drop the southern belle charm Norma Jean, and just tell Mrs. Deaton here the truth.

NORMA JEAN. The truth? You want the truth now, do you? Well the truth is that, as far as I am aware, all of my bay mates were counting sheep in their cot since lights out at ten. Under this roof we respect the bonds of sisterhood. And seeing as Miss Mildred here is a flight lieutenant and I am the Squadron Commander, I believe that my word outranks hers.

MRS. DEATON. Mildred?

MILDRED. She's right. Truth is I didn't know who they were, and I thought, if you had names…

MRS. DEATON.	**NORMA JEAN.**
I'm so sorry to disturb you at such a late hour, Squadron Commander Harris. *(she drags* **MILDRED** *offstage)* You are grounded until graduation, do you here me? You're lucky it's just breaking curfew we're getting you on, otherwise –	It's no trouble at all, Mrs. Deaton. I hope you get some sleep yourself soon. You too, Mildred.

NORMA JEAN. *(waits until they've left)* Lord forgive me, I don't think I've ever lasted in a lie so long.

VIRGINIA. That was marvelous!

ALICE. Well done, Norma Jean.

CAROL. You completely sewed Mildred Simmons' mouth shut!

NORMA JEAN. Good, her voice absolutely crawls me up a wall.

EDDIE. You didn't haveta do that. You could've turned me in.

NORMA JEAN. I know.

EDDIE. Thanks.

NORMA JEAN. Hey, I didn't do you any favors. Do you know how hard advanced training is going to be?

Scene Ten

(Lights. CAROL and ALICE at the well. MRS. DEATON alone. VIRGINIA writing.)

MRS. DEATON. Dear Mrs. Cochran, The class of 44-W-4 are three weeks into advanced training. Below are the names of the women we have lost over the past four months: Teddy Rolfe, washed. Millicent Scott, washed. Margaret Fort, washed.

VIRGINIA. *(to WILLIAM)* William, every morning I pray to God, saying: Please, please let me eat dinner in the same place as I did breakfast.

ALICE. *(shutting book)* I think that's enough studying for one day.

CAROL. No it's not, no it's not!

ALICE. You know, no one has ever washed out because they failed Ground School.

CAROL. And I don't plan to be the first.

ALICE. Fine. But I'm done with this book. Let's go look at a real-live engine.

(ALICE and CAROL exit.)

MRS. DEATON. Sylvia Meyer, washed. Helen Carter, washed. Nancy Hill, left for medical reasons. Libby James, washed. Helen Huff, washed. Jane Easton, washed. Betty Baughman, washed. Millicent Brown, washed. Susan Shaw, washed. Barbara Richards, washed.

VIRGINIA. Sometimes it feels like there is not a world outside of Sweetwater.

(EDDIE follows MILDRED on stage.)

EDDIE. Mildred! Was it you who put an alarm clock under my bed that woke me up at four this morning?

MILDRED. You put soap shavings and peanut shells in my bed covers!

NORMA JEAN. *(entering)* Edith Harknell, are you planning to play poker in our latrine again tonight?

EDDIE & MILDRED. What's it to you? You don't play.

(**EDDIE** and **MILDRED** exit, with **CAROL** chasing after.)

CAROL. Wait for me! Wait for me! I wanna play, I wanna play!

NORMA JEAN. I've got better things to do!

(counting on her fingers)

Hello James. All is good, no, no.

(restarts counting)

...all good here in Texas. I love, no, no.

(restarts counting)

...love flying the AT-6.

VIRGINIA. (to **WILLIAM**) Norma Jean got word that her James is alive in a prison in Japan, and they have been able to sneak messages back and forth through the Red Cross, as long as they are kept to twenty-five words.

MRS. DEATON. Phyllis Knight, washed. Wendy Turner, caught with alcohol, washed. Gretchen Collins, washed. Velma Sullivan, washed. Elizabeth Madison, washed. Isabel Houser, washed. Eleanor Johnson, washed.

(**ALICE** and **CAROL** cross the stage.)

ALICE. Mexican wine doesn't taste as good as Belgian wine.

CAROL. Yes, but we can't drive to Belgium.

VIRGINIA. (to **WILLIAM**) Carol got a "Dear Jane" letter from her fella in Japan, so she's been rather sullen, when she's not stealing a kiss from a mechanic named Hernandez in the hangar.

MRS. DEATON. Joan Handerson, washed. Lucy Turner, washed. Mary Ellen Snyder, washed. Jane Carmichael washed, and Rosalie Hartson –

VIRGINIA. It seems like someone washes every day. And the radio tells us men are dying every day. This morning my heart felt too heavy to fly. Will this war never end? Will you ever write me back? I hope so. Missing you, Virginia.

(**MRS. DEATON** *exits.*)

EDDIE. *(entering)* Heard from your folks lately?

VIRGINIA. My father found the letters I wrote Mother. He burned them. He has written me out of his will.

EDDIE. It's times like these when I'm glad I don't know where my father is.

VIRGINIA. Mother and I are going to get a PO Box and write in secret. Mother and I are good at secrets.

NORMA JEAN. You can't make complete sentences with only 25 words!

(**CAROL** *and* **ALICE** *enter.*)

ALICE. I call my mother back in Oregon every week. I'm afraid she'll forget me.

VIRGINIA. That's silly, how can a mother forget her own daughter?

CAROL. The problem comes the other way around.

NORMA JEAN. What's that supposed to mean?

CAROL. I don't remember my ma, and she left me.

NORMA JEAN. But Alice didn't leave a child, she left her mother... right?

CAROL. Oops.

ALICE. ...I have a five year old daughter. Her name is Ruby. She's back in Oregon, with my mom.

EDDIE. You've got a kid?

VIRGINIA. Why didn't you tell us?

NORMA JEAN. She's ashamed. Because there were plenty of women who were willing to come here that didn't have children waiting at home for them, but she left hers.

ALICE. I got the call to arms from Jackie Cochran; I felt like it was something that I was supposed to do.

NORMA JEAN. For yourself!

EDDIE. For her country! Norma Jean, why are you getting so upset about this?

NORMA JEAN. Before James left, we'd been trying. We've been trying for what seems like forever –

ALICE. I don't take her for granted, Norma Jean. I know what I've got. I know how good it is.

NORMA JEAN. I sure hope you do.

CAROL. Norma Jean –

NORMA JEAN. I can't tell you how many times I've thought that I would give up flying forever if God would just give me a child.

EDDIE. And if God were to come by here tomorrow and be willing to sign a contract to that effect, would you sign it now?

NORMA JEAN. Yes.

EDDIE. You would?

NORMA JEAN. Yes, I would.

EDDIE. Don't you lie to me, Ace!

NORMA JEAN. …Fine! I don't know! I don't know anymore.

EDDIE. None of us could. Because it's the not-knowing that gets us up in the morning!

(short beat)

They sent Ricky under cover. I might not hear from him for months.

VIRGINIA. William has not written since December.

ALICE. I haven't gotten a wine bottle from Roger since Christmas.

CAROL. I haven't kissed Hernandez in a few hours. He tells me we can't be together, and then he kisses me. I don't get it.

ALICE. Honey, you can do better than Hernandez.

ZIGGIE. *(entering)* Attention! Time for Night Flying.

(Lights. The WOMEN move to their flight positions. CAROL exits.)

ZIGGIE. You will wait on the flight line starting at dark, and fly until two or three some nights.

Mom, your favorite cafeteria cook, will bring us coffee and small sandwiches to have while we wait our turn. It's a miracle we haven't had any accidents; we've only oil lamps burning the length of the runway to see by.

VIRGINIA. How could I describe flight to you, William? It's vibration. It's sensation. When you take off...it's power. You push the throttle forward and it pushes back and you go on up, and it's beautiful up there. You would think it would be loud, but it's not. Sound is vacuumed out, like when you are submerged under water, and the world takes on a simple grace. The earth is alive, Will; it moves under us, it exhales. I cannot shake this feeling that when I am in the air, God is holding me in the palm of Her hand.

Scene Eleven

(Lights. CAROL *enters with a parachute; other* WOMEN *help her secure it. She moves to her flight position as other* WOMEN *sing the first verse of "Blood in the Cockpit" to an up-tempo tune of "Blood on the Saddle.")*

WOMEN.
PITY THE PILOT, ALL BLOODY AND GORE
FOR SHE WON' BE FLYING THE PATTERN NO MORE!

*(*WOMEN *address the audience.)*

VIRGINIA. William, there was a lot of excitement in Sweetwater today.

EDDIE. It was an accident, Ziggie. Honest.

ALICE. I don't care if visiting hours are over, Dr. Monsrud, I want to see Carol.

VIRGINIA. Carol was doing aerobatic tricks, which we're not supposed to do.

NORMA JEAN. I watched the whole thing, Mrs. Deaton, and it's a miracle she's alive.

VIRGINIA. One guess who taught her aerobatics.

EDDIE. Ricky taught me some back when we barnstormed, and I swear they calm me down, but I should've figured Shrimp's adrenaline would hit her faster than it might me. She's so dang small.

CAROL. That's it, come on girl, you've got it. You've got it.

NORMA JEAN. Carol isn't Carol unless she's doing something without thinking.

CAROL. Whoo! Ha-ha, ah! Yaaaaa – hhhooooo!

ALICE. If she's awake, she'll want to see me.

VIRGINIA. A mechanic left a rag on her plane engine. It caught fire.

CAROL. Aw dammit, dammit, think, Carol THINK! *(pressing buttons)* no, still spinning upside down. *(pulling a lever)* AHHH that ground is really close! Where's the eject button, where is it?! Gottcha, you son of a –

VIRGINIA. Ejecting from a plane is a last resort.

NORMA JEAN. Are you aware, Mrs. Deaton, that we've never gotten more instruction than a cartoon pamphlet on how to bail?

EDDIE. You taught us to count to ten before hitting the silk, otherwise you're chopped liver, and she knew that...

VIRGINIA. But the ground was too close, so she had to improvise.

CAROL. ONE-TEN!

(Lights out on **CAROL** *as she pulls the ripcord.)*

VIRGINIA. Thank goodness she only got bruises for her trouble.

ALICE. Will you at least make sure she gets some avocados with her dinner tonight? They're her favorite.

NORMA JEAN & EDDIE. I could kill Shrimp for doing something so stupid –

EDDIE. without me! I'm supposed to be the hot pilot around here.

NORMA JEAN. Maybe you're getting smart in your old age, Eddie.

EDDIE. I've got to stop hanging around you. Responsibility is contagious.

Scene Twelve

(Lights. **WOMEN** *at the well. The sound of a plane overhead.)*

VIRGINIA. I love that sound. I can't stand long silences much anymore.

EDDIE. Who are you writing?

VIRGINIA. William.

ALICE. I thought he hadn't written in a month or two.

VIRGINIA. I got one this morning. A short one.

NORMA JEAN. I told you he'd come around.

VIRGINIA. In the letter, he said: "This flying business is a phase that I'm willing to indulge until you come home and be my girl again."

NORMA JEAN. That's not quite coming around.

EDDIE. He said that? He's an ass.

VIRGINIA & NORMA JEAN. Eddie!

EDDIE. What? Correct me if I'm wrong, but this guy didn't want you to come here, he waited until December to say he wanted to see you, and then when you couldn't get there because of a Texan snowstorm, he goes back to giving you the silent treatment until finally he writes to say that? Doesn't he know you at all?

VIRGINIA. Of course he does. We grew up together.

EDDIE. Let me tell you something Virginia: when my mama married my daddy, he let her fly all over the God-damn state, but as soon as she had Ricky and me, he moved us closer to Jacksonville and he made her stop. And four years later, she got sick, and three years after that she was dead. And then Daddy ran off, because he couldn't stand us knowing the truth; that sickness wasn't what killed Mama, he was.

NORMA JEAN. Edith Harknell, you're scaring the girl!

EDDIE. Good. Kid should be living with her eyes wide open. Any one of these days could be our last, Shrimp here fell outta the sky two weeks ago –

CAROL. I'm never gonna hear the end of that, am I?

EDDIE. So you better be careful, is all I'm saying!

NORMA JEAN. Eddie, what's gotten into you?

EDDIE. Nothing, I'm fine.

ALICE. Virginia is nothing like your mother, Eddie.

(to **VIRGINIA***)*

Right?

(sound of a plane flying overhead)

VIRGINIA. Law number six: the women we are now is what matters. Not who we were before...even if we might have to go back to being those women when this is all over.

Scene Thirteen

(Lights. **WOMEN** *remain at well.* **ZIGGIE** *at one flight position, and* **MILDRED** *at another.)*

(She sings "I Wanna Be a Miss H.P.")

MILDRED.
I WANNA BE A MISS H.P.
H'MMMMM AND A LIL BIT MORE!
I WANNA BE A WASP TRAINEE,
H'MMMMM AND A LIL BIT MORE!
I WANNA BE A GRADUATE, AND THEN I'LL ASK NO MORE!
FOR ALL I'LL HAVE ALL THAT'S COMING TO ME,
HMM, AND A LIL BIT
HMM, AND A LIL BIT
HMM, AND A LIL BIT MORE!

ZIGGIE. Decision Height: the altitude at which a pilot must decide to descend for her landing or continue on and deem it a "missed approach."

(Lights. Sound of crash. A trumpet plays "Amazing Grace." **MRS. DEATON** *enters with microphone.)*

MRS. DEATON. At fifteen-hundred hours today Mary Stine, class 44-W-6, along with her instructor Ziggie Lewis, and Mildred Simmons, class 44-W-4 died in a mid-air collision. A memorial service will be held in the gym tomorrow morning. The Avenger Choir, started by Mildred, will sing a selection of hymns. A collection is being taken to help send Mildred and Mary home to their families. Ziggie, who had no family, will be laid to rest here at Avenger Field, where she was happiest.

Scene Fourteen

(Lights. The last morning of advanced training.)

(Asterisks [*] denote overlap in dialogue between two characters.)

(WOMEN *are in a ready room; the radio is on. We hear:)*

FEMALE CORPORAL. *(voice over)* Yes, they're allowed to have dates, but they must go out in groups of at least four, and they can't have dates with officers. The girls hit it off* very well with their brother soldiers, and they've already met some enlisted men they used to know back home. They're very careful of us out in this man's country though, which is alright with us.

HOST 1. *(voice over)* Who takes up with the guards?

FEMALE CORPORAL. *(voice over)* Captain, don't worry.

EDDIE*. I'm sure they have.

VIRGINIA. You're just jealous that you're not out in the Pacific with them.

EDDIE. You bet I am. I'd love to be there, in the thick of things. I'd beat up Carol's bull-riding Ben while I was at it.

HOST 1. *(voice over)* Alright. What's your particular job, ah, Corporal Hamilton?

FEMALE CORPORAL. *(voice over)* I'm a motor driver, *anything from a two and a half ton truck on down to a Jeep. We came out here to relieve men to go on active duty, and it's really happening.

NORMA JEAN*. Why are you jealous of this woman? You're the one flying, she's driving a Jeep!

EDDIE. But she's a corporal. She's *there*, doing something!

FEMALE CORPORAL. *(voice over)* I'm glad to say that the man whose place I have taken, has already received his orders to go.

HOST 1. *(voice over)* And that's one* of the newly arrived air WACS in the Pacific, Corporal Leah Hamilton, now taking a male truck driver's place, in the combat zone.[1] This is Weverly Edwards, out of Central Pacific Airfield, returning you to admiral radio, in New York.

NORMA JEAN*. She's doing the same thing we are: Freeing up a man to fight.

CAROL. *(entering with mail and a list)* I've got the mail and the list! For our army check rides, to move on to basic training…

I've got Lieutenant Baker, hangar one, Virginia and Eddie, you've both got Lieutenant Reinhart, hangar one, Norma Jean's got Second Lieutenant Foster, hangar two and…

ALICE. I got Captain Maytag, didn't I?

CAROL. In hangar one.

ALICE. I had a feeling.

CAROL. What do you mean?

ALICE. I can't explain it…last night I had a *feeling* I wasn't gonna last another night here. I think I'm going to wash.

NORMA JEAN. You can't know that, you're not God.

CAROL. Yeah, you are not going anywhere, not if we've got any say in it.

ALICE. That's all very nice, but –

CAROL. No buts! You'll just jinx yourself.

ALICE. No one has made it past Maytag, not since we've been here.

CAROL. But you're not "no one", you're Alice Hawkins, first to solo! Just throw a coin in the well on your way out to the flight line and keep cool. Here, take my penny.

ALICE. If you say so, Carol.

CAROL. Virginia, you got a letter from Rosalie!

VIRGINIA. *(opens it, excited)* She's teaching flute! To kids in the middle of her folks cornfield. She says if we ever

---

1 The radio broadcast should continue at a lower sound level for rest of scene, with the **WOMEN** not paying mind to it.

do a cross country trip up that way we should stop by. She gave us her coordinates.

EDDIE. Dang it, where did my lighter get to?

NORMA JEAN. You can fly without your lighter, Eddie.

EDDIE. Ricky gave me that lighter, I never go in the air without it.

NORMA JEAN. Stop being so superstitious.

EDDIE. Stop being so, un-superstitious.

CAROL. Norma Jean, here's one from James.

NORMA JEAN. *(opens it, reads)* Oh Lord. He doesn't think he'll be able to stomach meat again. He's eating dogs and rats.

CAROL. Eddie, there's one here for...never mind.

EDDIE. That for me? Who is it from? Shrimp!

CAROL. It's nothing, read it after your test.

EDDIE. Shrimp, leggo of it, just give it to me!

(EDDIE *opens the envelope, and reads. In the silence, the radio is audible again, and we hear:)*

MALE LIEUTENANT. *(voice over)* ...and now and then you'd see a big flash of fire and a ball of flame would drop into the sea. About 17 of them were shot down.

HOST 2. *(voice over)* Well, how about the raid itself, Jim?

MALE LIEUTENANT. *(voice over)* Well, the fighters went in first –

(CAROL *quickly turns radio off.* EDDIE, *stunned, hands the telegram to* NORMA JEAN.)

NORMA JEAN. *(opens, reads the telegram)* The Army Air Force deeply regrets to inform you that your brother Richard M. Harknell airmen was killed in action while in the performance of his duties and service of his country on seventh March in Germany.

(short beat)

Oh Eddie.

(**NORMA JEAN** *goes to comfort* **EDDIE,** *but steps on something. She picks it up.*)

Found your lighter.

(*She presses it into* **EDDIE***'s hand.*)

Now let's get to flying. There's a war on.

(*Lights.* **ALICE** *moves to her flight position.* **WOMEN** *march and sing "I'm A Flying Wreck."*)

CAROL, VIRGINIA, NORMA JEAN.
> I'M A FLYING WRECK A RISKIN' MY NECK,
> AND A HELLOFA PILOT TOO!
> A HELLOFA, HELLOFA, HELLOFA, HELLOFA, HELLOFA PILOT,
> TOO!
> LIKE ALL THE JOLLY GOOD FLYERS,
> THE GREMLINS TREAT ME MEAN,
> I'M A FLYIN' WRECK, A RISKIN' MY NECK FOR THE GOOD OLE
> 318TH!

ALICE. *(at flight position)*
> WHEN THAT THIN-AND-BLONDE CAPTAIN COMES
> TO VIEW US IN OUR DRILL,
> WE'LL DO A FOUR WINDS MARCH, SIR,
> AND CHECK OUT O'ER THE HILL,
> AND WHEN HE CALLS ATTENTION!
> WE'LL CLICK OUR HEELS AND YELL,
> "I'M JUST A RAW CIVILIAN, SIR, AND YOU CAN GO TO HELL!

CAROL, VIRGINIA, NORMA JEAN.
> I'M A FLYING WRECK A RISKIN' MY NECK,
> AND A HELLOFA PILOT TOO!
> A HELLOFA, HELLOFA, HELLOFA, HELLOFA, HELLOFA PILOT,
> TOO!
> LIKE ALL THE JOLLY GOOD FLYERS,
> THE GREMLINS TREAT ME MEAN,
> I'M A FLYIN' WRECK, A RISKIN' MY NECK FOR THE GOOD OLE
> 3L8TH!

(*Lights. In the ready room, after:*)

CAROL. You did it Alice, you did it! Victory over Captain Maytag!

NORMA JEAN. And you thought you would be rid of us. You wish!

VIRGINIA. You should have seen the look on his face, Alice, when you got off. It was like it was killing him to sign your pass slip.

CAROL. They should knock that Fifinella off that sign and put a big ole' picture of you on top!

ALICE. Quit it, that's enough flattery for one evening. How's Eddie doing?

(**NORMA JEAN** *shakes her head.*)

ALICE. That bad?

CAROL. She's smoking a whole lot.

VIRGINIA. Lieutenant Reinhart sent her away when she tried to take her check-ride. He's making her take it tomorrow.

MRS. DEATON. *(entering)* Mrs. Hawkins, you have a phone call in my office.

ALICE. But it's not Saturday – is everything alright? Is my Ruby okay?

MRS. DEATON. It's not your daughter on the line. It's your husband.

ALICE. Roger? My Roger's on the line?

(**ALICE** *runs off,* **MRS. DEATON** *following.*)

NORMA JEAN. I guess she's gonna leave us after all.

Scene Fifteen

(Lights. A few hours later. CAROL *and* VIRGINIA *wait by the well.)*

VIRGINIA. Mrs. Deaton told me Congress is holding a hearing next month, to decide if we get militarized.

CAROL. What does that mean?

VIRGINIA. It means we would no longer be civilians, but a legitimate part of the military. Can you imagine? William and my father would have to take us seriously if the bill passes.

CAROL. They'll never take us seriously if pilots like Alice choose to go home.

VIRGINIA. Careful, you are starting to sound like Eddie.

*(*NORMA JEAN *enters with* ALICE, *who is dressed in her civvies and carrying her suitcase.)*

CAROL. *(to* ALICE*)* So Roger's back?

ALICE. With one less eyeball, yes.

VIRGINIA. That's so sad. He will never get to fly again.

ALICE. He's alive and he's back with me, Virginia. I can't ask for more than that.

NORMA JEAN. No, you can't.

ALICE. Norma Jean –

NORMA JEAN. Oh, don't you worry about me. Safe travels back to Oregon.

VIRGINIA. I am going to miss you.

ALICE. Do me a favor: keep Norma Jean and Eddie from killing each other.

*(*EDDIE *enters.)*

ALICE. Eddie...

EDDIE. You're so close. You left your family, your daughter, to see this through...for what?

ALICE. He's home, Eddie.

EDDIE. And he's asking for you? Needs you back home to keep his castle? When he's around, do you just shut your brain off and let him make all your decisions?

ALICE. How dare you – !

EDDIE. You're leaving out of duty, aren't you?

ALICE.	**NORMA JEAN.**
No, I – !	Eddie, stop this!

EDDIE. Because the woman who just kicked Maytag's ass, she's not done.

ALICE. I am done! I promised Ruby that when her Daddy came home, her family would be together again.

EDDIE. You can't use your daughter as an excuse to quit!

ALICE. I'm not quitting, I'm choosing! I'm choosing my daughter over wings.

(**EDDIE**, *clearly shaken, exits.* **NORMA JEAN** *follows after her.* **VIRGINIA** *gives* **ALICE** *one last hug before exiting.*)

CAROL. Who'll lead the march to breakfast, if you're gone?

ALICE. You. If you'll accept the position.

CAROL. I guess I could do that. Might be hard though. Because I'm so small.

ALICE. You're not that small.

CAROL. No I am, but I don't mind, really. It was great as a kid, I could hide really well. Ma and Pa fought a lot. I'd ride one of our horses down our road, just to get outta there, but I'd always get to the point where I wasn't allowed any further. The road forks, and Ma was worried that I'd get lost, so she told me when I saw the fork to always turn around and come back. One day, I was seven, I was sitting at that fork, wishing I could find a way to go farther, when I heard a rumbling. It was a plane, flying overhead of me, and out past the fork. I watched it until I couldn't see it anymore. And I got so excited, I rushed home to tell my Ma we could leave Oklahoma, I'd found a way to go farther...but when I got home, I found her room all bare and the family car gone. She'd left, didn't even say goodbye.

(*short beat*)

I'm happy for Ruby, I'm sure she's been missing you something fierce, but you're my best and I'm gonna miss... I'm gonna miss –

ALICE. When all this is over, come stay with us in Oregon.

CAROL. Roger –

ALICE. Honey, he doesn't get a choice... Now, are you going walk me to the main gate or not?

CAROL. Sure.

(in regards to the well)

Wait! Don't you want to say goodbye?

ALICE. I am saying goodbye, Carol. With each step forward I am saying goodbye.

*(**ALICE** holds **CAROL***'s hand as they exit.)*

Scene Sixteen

(Lights. The runway, early on Easter morning.
VIRGINIA, **CAROL**, *and* **MRS. DEATON** *stand singing
the hymn "The Strife is O'er, the Battle Done."* **NORMA
JEAN** *stands separate.)*

NORMA JEAN. *(counting on her fingers)* Basic Training started.
Cross country flights long and hard, no, no…flights
tiring. Today Easter morning, airfield sunrise service.
Sang "Victory."

WOMEN.
THE STRIFE IS O'ER, THE BATTLE DONE,
NOW IS THE VICTOR'S TRIUMPH WON
NOW BE THE SONG OF PRAISE BEGUN
ALLELUIA!

NORMA JEAN. *(counting on fingers)* You never guess who
came.

*(**EDDIE** enters, and takes **NORMA JEAN**'s hand.)*

WOMEN.
ALLELUIA, ALLELUIA, ALLELUIA!

*(Lights. **MRS. DEATON** exits one way, **EDDIE** and
NORMA JEAN another. **CAROL** and **VIRGINIA** address
the audience.)*

VIRGINIA. William, there is nothing basic about Basic
Training.

CAROL. Dear Monsters: You can't see the ground in a
BT-13, you just got instruments and your wits to keep
you on course. I am great at it! I'm already used to
flying blind.

VIRGINIA. The Army Air Force keeps the good planes
for the men, so most of ours are in poor shape: the
BT-13's are the worst. I swear, these buckets of bolts
only got duct tape, chewing gum, and prayers keeping
them together.

CAROL. It's a thrill to fly high above the highways, and not
be able to see a damn thing but the sky.
I'll send another postcard soon – we fly next to
California!

VIRGINIA. I have been to Alabama, Georgia, and Missouri so far. To think, six months ago I had never left Connecticut.

EDDIE. *(entering, to* **CAROL***)* You know Shrimp, I think Ricky would go berserk if he saw me flying cross country. I take my top off and sunbath.

(They share a laugh.)

VIRGINIA. We'll soon be assigned to different bases, to ferry planes, so it's important for us to practice cross country flights. They are nerve-wracking. It's impossible to keep each other in sight, so you are mostly alone. And if you're lucky, and have no problems and make it to your destination base on time…then you have to wait for everyone else.

(Lights. The three wait silently on the runway, eyes glued to the horizon. **NORMA JEAN** *finally enters.)*

CAROL. Norma Jean!

VIRGINIA. Thank goodness.

EDDIE. What took you so long!

NORMA JEAN. What, I'm a little late, and you all stand here like a couple of nervous mothers? Isn't that my job?

EDDIE. Shut up Ace.

*(***EDDIE*** *scoops* **NORMA JEAN** *up in a bear hug. Has* **EDDIE***'s casing finally cracked?)*

VIRGINIA. Graduation is looming like a Texas dust storm, William, and I am terrified. The thought of leaving my friends and this place should make me feel excited. I'll finally get to do what I came here to do – be a part of the war effort! But instead, I feel such grief. We all feel it, but we try not to talk about it. It is the B-29 in the room, you might say. Instead, we watch each other fly from the runway. We relish the taste of butter on our morning toast. We continue the delusion that Sweetwater is forever; we know in our hearts it is too good to last. I'm beginning to fear that maybe you and I are too. Tell me I'm wrong? Signed, Virginia.

Scene Seventeen

(Lights. Early morning, the day of their last cross country trip. WOMEN cross the stage towards the well. They hear something, and hide.)

EDDIE. Shh!

CAROL. They're going to catch us. They're going to catch us, and we're going to get kicked out before we can graduate next week!

NORMA JEAN. They sure will if you don't shut your mouth!

(EDDIE strips to her underwear and steps in.)

EDDIE. It's like bath water.

(She sits in the well. The others follow her lead.)

CAROL. This feels better than sleeping.

EDDIE. This feels better than smoking.

NORMA JEAN. This feels better than church!

VIRGINIA. Today's our last cross country till graduation, can you believe that?... Where do you think we'll go?

EDDIE. After graduation?

CAROL. I wanna get assigned to Casper Air Field, in Wyoming. Or some other base with mountains.

NORMA JEAN. I'd like to be assigned to Camp Davis. That's only a few hours from my folks.

EDDIE. I don't care where they send me, I just wanna volunteer for a top-secret project. They have those, you know.

CAROL. When the war's over, I'm gonna live in the mountains.

NORMA JEAN. When James gets home, we're going to have a baby.

EDDIE. Maybe I'll barnstorm around the country again, just one more time.

CAROL. When I've got enough money, I'll buy a ranch of my own, with horses and dogs.

NORMA JEAN. We will name her Jackie, and we'll teach her how to fly.

EDDIE. I hear they're training women to be officers. I could be the New Ziggie Lewis!

CAROL. Oregon has mountains, right?

NORMA JEAN. Yes, Carol. *(short beat)* What about you, Virginia?

EDDIE. Yeah, when are you and Will getting hitched?

CAROL. Whose gonna to be your maid of honor? Can I do it?

EDDIE. No Shrimp, she's going to ask Rosalie. Or me.

NORMA JEAN. Virginia? What's going on in that pretty little head of yours?

VIRGINIA. I was just thinking, about how many people the war has taken, how many more it will take before it's over. I'm prepared to do whatever it takes until then. But when it is over, I'm going to see the Pacific Ocean.... No, I don't want to just see it, I want to swim in it. And fish in it, and sail over it, and watch the sun sink into it.

NORMA JEAN. Time to go.

(They step out of the well; hearing a sound, they run off, bursting.)

Scene Eighteen

(A few hours later, in the hanger. The deafening sounds of numerous propellers and engines, gearing up in pre-flight.)

(MRS. DEATON addresses the audience.)

MRS. DEATON. *(with her microphone)* Now remember girls, take care to complete your entire checklist for pre-flight, to bring with you the correct maps, and for any of you who find you need a cushion or two to sit on to reach all of the buttons, that you acquire one in the hangar. You are to take no pit stops to grandparents houses, make no detours to go fence hopping.

You fly directly to Douglas Army Air Field in Arizona, fuel up, and then off directly to Minter Field in California! Have a safe cross country flight girls; we'll see you on Sunday.

(WOMEN run on in flight gear, searching for their planes.)

EDDIE. Mine is all the way at the bottom of the hangar.

VIRGINIA. *(exiting)* That's me over there!

CAROL. *(exiting)* See you in California!

NORMA JEAN. *(taking a wine bottle from her bag)* Eddie, wait! Alice sent this wine to me. See, it's from Oregon? I thought we could all drink it in California tonight, with no Mrs. Deaton to catch us.

EDDIE. What do you want me to do with it? I've got no room on my plane, same as you.

NORMA JEAN. I'm the squadron commander, Eddie, I can't fly with it.

EDDIE. Fine.

NORMA JEAN. *(kissing EDDIE on the cheek)* Thank you!

(EDDIE exits.)

CAROL. *(entering)* Norma Jean! I forgot my map!

NORMA JEAN. What?

CAROL. I don't know how, but I did, I left it on my cot all the way back in the bay!

NORMA JEAN. Which plane is yours?

CAROL. That one over there. With the mechanics crawling all over it? They said it won't be ready for another fifteen minutes.

NORMA JEAN. Alright, you go and take my plane and my map. Seeing as I got to make sure everyone gets off the ground before I can go anywhere, I'll go back and get your map and take your plane.

CAROL. Are you sure?

NORMA JEAN. Of course I'm sure! Don't get lost now, I don't want to hunt you down in Louisiana like last time.

CAROL. *(exiting)* I promise! I promise!

*(**NORMA JEAN** moves to flight position, singing lyrics from "You'll Go Forth.")*

NORMA JEAN.
LEAVE YOUR INSTRUMENT LORE TO POOR W-4
LEAVE YOUR INSTRUMENT LORE TO POOR W-4
YOU CAN LEAVE ALL THE LINKS WITH THEIR GADGETS GALORE
'CAUSE YOU AIN'T GONNA BE HERE NO LONGER.

YOU'LL GO FORTH FROM HERE WITH YOUR SILVER WINGS
YOU'LL GO FORTH FROM HERE WITH YOUR SILVER WINGS
SANTIAGO BLUE AND A HEART THAT SINGS
'CAUSE YOU AIN'T GONNA BE HERE NO LONGER!

(Lights. Sound of a plane, descending; of fire, burning.)

Scene Nineteen

(Graduation morning. **EDDIE,** **CAROL,** *and* **VIRGINIA** *at the well.* **EDDIE** *holds the wine bottle* **NORMA JEAN** *gave her in the previous scene; they each take a sip, but only the one.)*

EDDIE. Dang, Alice knows how to buy good wine.

VIRGINIA. It was nice, Eddie, that they let you escort her home. I thought they wouldn't let you, it was so close to graduation.

EDDIE. They couldn't've stopped me if they'd tried.

CAROL. What did her parents say? Her sisters?

EDDIE. Not much. They gave me the telegram that the government sent them.

VIRGINIA. What did it say?

*(**EDDIE** hands her the telegram.)*

(reading the telegram)

Your daughter was killed this evening. Where do you want us to ship the body?

CAROL. That's all it says? Lemme see.

VIRGINIA. It says nothing about how…or why…

EDDIE. *(taking telegram back)* Nope.

VIRGINIA. Gosh. Is that all we are to them? Just, bodies?

CAROL. This is my fault. If I had just remembered my map…

VIRGINIA. It was not your fault, Carol. Even if you had remembered, she still would have made you take her plane.

EDDIE. She would've.

VIRGINIA. She would have wanted to be the last one to leave.

EDDIE. We switch planes all the time.

VIRGINIA. It was not your fault.

CAROL. I know. But I still can't stop thinking…

VIRGINIA. I bet her James was at those pearly gates to meet her. Can you imagine? Dying the same day as your husband when he's half-a-world away?

EDDIE. She didn't want to. Doc said she broke her hands pounding on the door, trying to get out.

VIRGINIA. They say God opens all doors to those who knock, but I guess she didn't bother opening that one.

CAROL. ... Did you just say "she?"

VIRGINIA. You never heard Norma Jean's theory? She told me once that she liked to think of God as a woman. Isn't that just, the most...

CAROL. The most outrageous...

EDDIE. The most bizarre...

VIRGINIA. ...the most marvelous thing you ever heard?

(short beat)

I miss her.

EDDIE. They're probably lining up without us.

CAROL. *(exiting)* They can't do that! I've got to lead the march!

VIRGINIA. I don't want to leave, Eddie. I don't want to stop being this person.

EDDIE. So don't....C'mon Kid, you know what Norma Jean'd say if she were here. "Now let's get to flying."

EDDIE & VIRGINIA. "There's a war on."

(EDDIE places the wine bottle on the well wall, exits.)

Scene Twenty

(Lights.)

VIRGINIA. William... Graduation was a lovely ceremony. Mother was beaming so brightly she might have been the sun.

(ZIGGIE LEWIS enters with a camera.)

ZIGGIE. Why do you fly?

VIRGINIA. We have gotten our assignments and Carol and I head out to Camp Davis, North Carolina soon.

(CAROL enters the space, regards VIRGINIA.)

ZIGGIE. Do you love heights?

VIRGINIA. But first we're going to visit Rosalie in Iowa.

ZIGGIE. Do you love speed?

VIRGINIA. And then we will drop Eddie off at her base in Dayton, Ohio.

ZIGGIE. Do you enjoy pretending to be one of God's angels, soaring up and around the clouds?

(NORMA JEAN enters the space, regards VIRGINIA.)

VIRGINIA. I am having trouble sleeping. I close my eyes and I see the runway in California. I see the towering mountains red in the sunset and I see Eddie.

(EDDIE enters, looking out, waiting.)

Her eyes on the skyline, waiting for a plane.

ZIGGIE. Are you attempting to escape a small life?

(ROSALIE enters the space, regards VIRGINIA.)

VIRGINIA. I hear the young lieutenant say, "Someone spotted smoke in the mountains, and a burning plane has been found."

ZIGGIE. Do you fly to see what's beyond the horizon?

(ALICE enters the space, regards VIRGINIA.)

VIRGINIA. "The girl landed it well," he said, "but the latch was broken on her cockpit door; she didn't have a chance." Eddie only looks at him long enough to say, "She was a woman, not a girl." Then I watch Eddie Harknell cry for the first time.

ZIGGIE. Do you fly because you feel heavy?

(EDDIE now regards VIRGINIA.)

VIRGINIA. I am telling you this because I have been thinking for a long time: If I were at decision height, and I chose to land, who would I want waiting for me at the end of the runway? I used to think it'd be you. But now?

ZIGGIE. Are you seeking another kind of baptism?

(As each woman is named, they move to stand on the well wall.)

VIRGINIA. Eddie, Carol, Rosalie, Alice, even Norma Jean... they are continuing on. They are not quite ready to land, and neither am I. Perhaps when the war's over, we can meet each other again as new people. Until then, I'll be flying as Virginia Hascall, Woman Airforce Service Pilot.

(VIRGINIA salutes, then turns and joins women on the well wall. VIRGINIA throws herself into the well with complete confidence. The other WOMEN join her and a celebration erupts.)

(ZIGGIE takes a picture; camera flashes, blackout.)

End of Play

ENSEMBLE APPENDIX

This appendix is for the use of productions employing an ensemble. The appendix includes "new" marching songs that the playwright requests the ensemble sing in specific scene transitions, as well as a list of recommended songs/ scenes that a production might use ensemble members for as well.

MARCHING SONG: END OF SCENE TWO

ZIGGIE. Do you accept, Miss Hawkins?

ALICE. *(exchanging a look with* **NORMA JEAN***)* It's Mrs. Hawkins, and yes, I do.

(The **WOMEN** *and* **ZIGGIE** *exit as ensemble march to "Deep in the Heart of Texas" as we transition back to the bay.)*

WOMEN.
> WE DAMN NEAR FREEZE IN THOSE OPEN PT'S
> XXXX DEEP IN THE HEART OF TEXAS.
> WE'RE NEVER AT EASE IN THESE BIG BT'S
> XXXX DEEP IN THE HEART OF TEXAS.
> IF YOU DON'T LOCK THE LATCH, YOU'LL FALL OUT OF THE
>   HATCH
> XXXX DEEP IN THE HEART OF TEXAS.
> IF YOU DON'T RELAX, YOU'LL BE IN AIR FACTS
> XXXX DEEP IN THE HEART OF TEXAS.

MARCHING SONG: END OF SCENE NINE

EDDIE. Thanks.

NORMA JEAN. Hey, I didn't do you any favors. Do you know how hard advanced training is going to be?

(Lights. **ENSEMBLE** *march on, singing "Roll out the airplanes" as we transition out of the bay.)*

WOMEN.

> ROLL OUT THE AIRPLANES! WE GOT A BIG JOB TO DO.
> ROLL OUT THE AIRPLANES! HURRY, SO WE CAN GET
>   THROUGH.
> WE'LL PRACTICE SEQUENCE WHEN WE GO UP EVERY DAY,
> JUST SO WE CAN FERRY AIRPLANES FOR THE U. S. A.!

MARCHING SONG: TOP OF SCENE EIGHTEEN

(A few hours later, in the hanger. The deafening sounds of numerous propellers and engines, gearing up in pre-flight. **ENSEMBLE** *march on, singing the chorus of "You'll Go Forth":)*

WOMEN.

> YOU'LL GO FORTH FROM HERE WITH YOUR SILVER WINGS
> YOU'LL GO FORTH FROM HERE WITH YOUR SILVER WINGS
> SANTIAGO BLUE AND A HEART THAT SINGS
> 'CAUSE YOU AIN'T GONNA BE HERE NO LONGER!

*(***MRS. DEATON*** addresses the audience.)*

PLAYWRIGHT RECOMMENDS ENSEMBLE PARTICIPATION IN:

"Yankee Doodle Pilot" in Scene Three (in lieu of using principals).

"I Wanna Be a Miss H.P." in the transition between Scenes Four and Five.

"Gee Ma, I Wanna Go Home" in Scene Seven; they should exit with MILDRED after the last chorus of the song is sung.

"I'm a Flying Wreck" in Scene Fifteen.

"The Strife is O'er, the Battle Done" in Scene Sixteen.

"You'll Go Forth" (first verse only) at the end of Scene Eighteen.